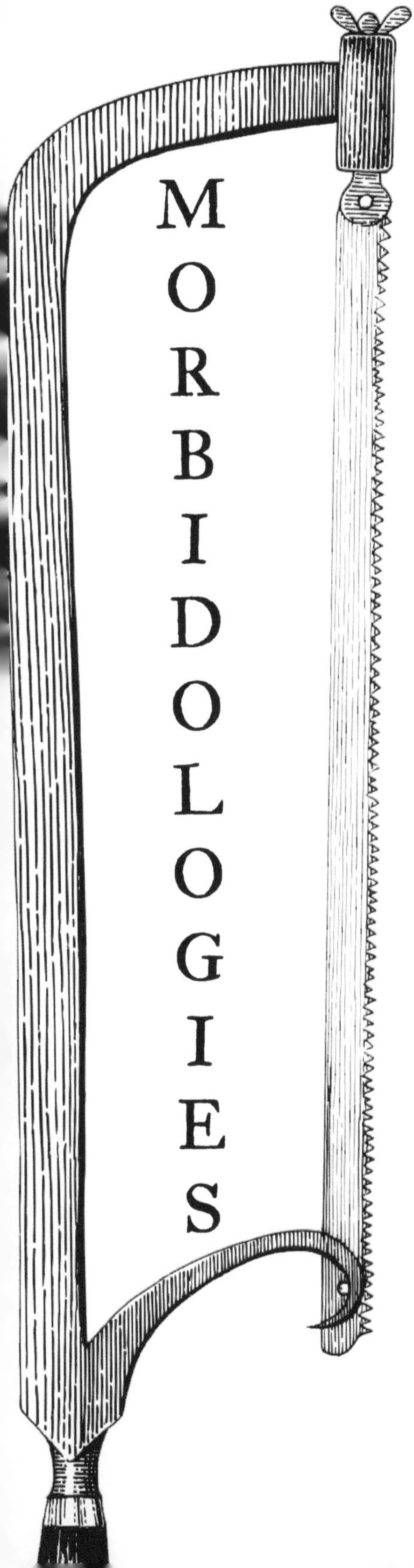

MORBIDOLOGIES

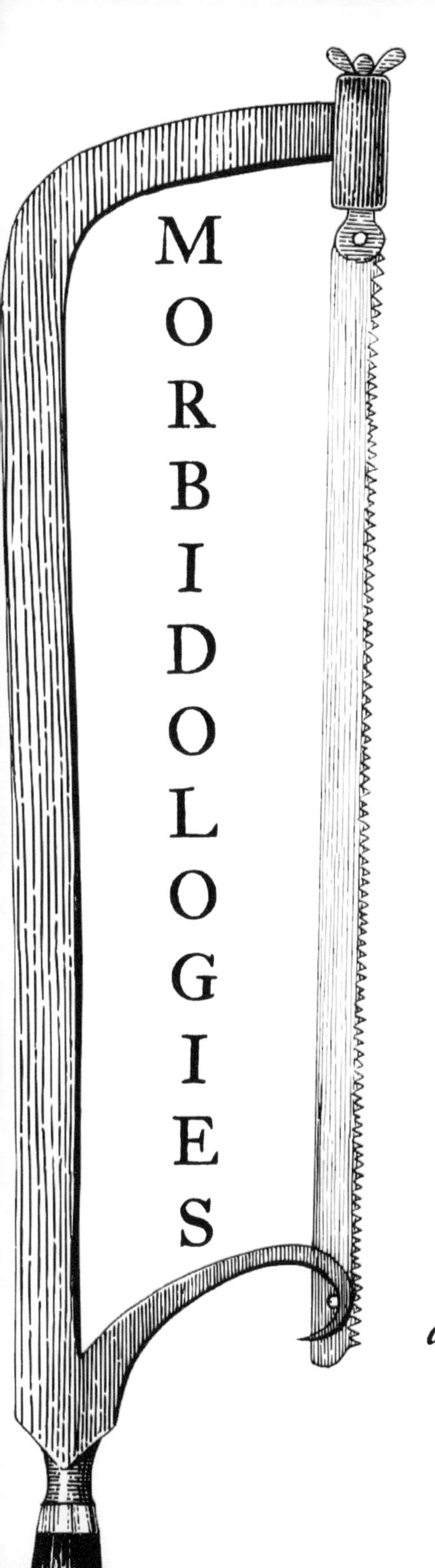

MORBIDOLOGIES

EDITED BY

SHANE D. KEENE

and JOHN F.D. TAFF

Morbidologies

ISBN: 979-8218232917
Cover art & design by Christine M. Scott | Clever Crow Consulting & Design
Interior design & formatting by Todd Keisling | Dullington Design Co.

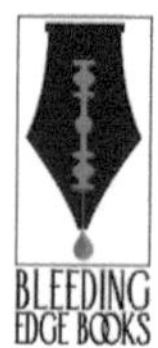

Bleeding Edge Books
www.bleedingedgepub.com

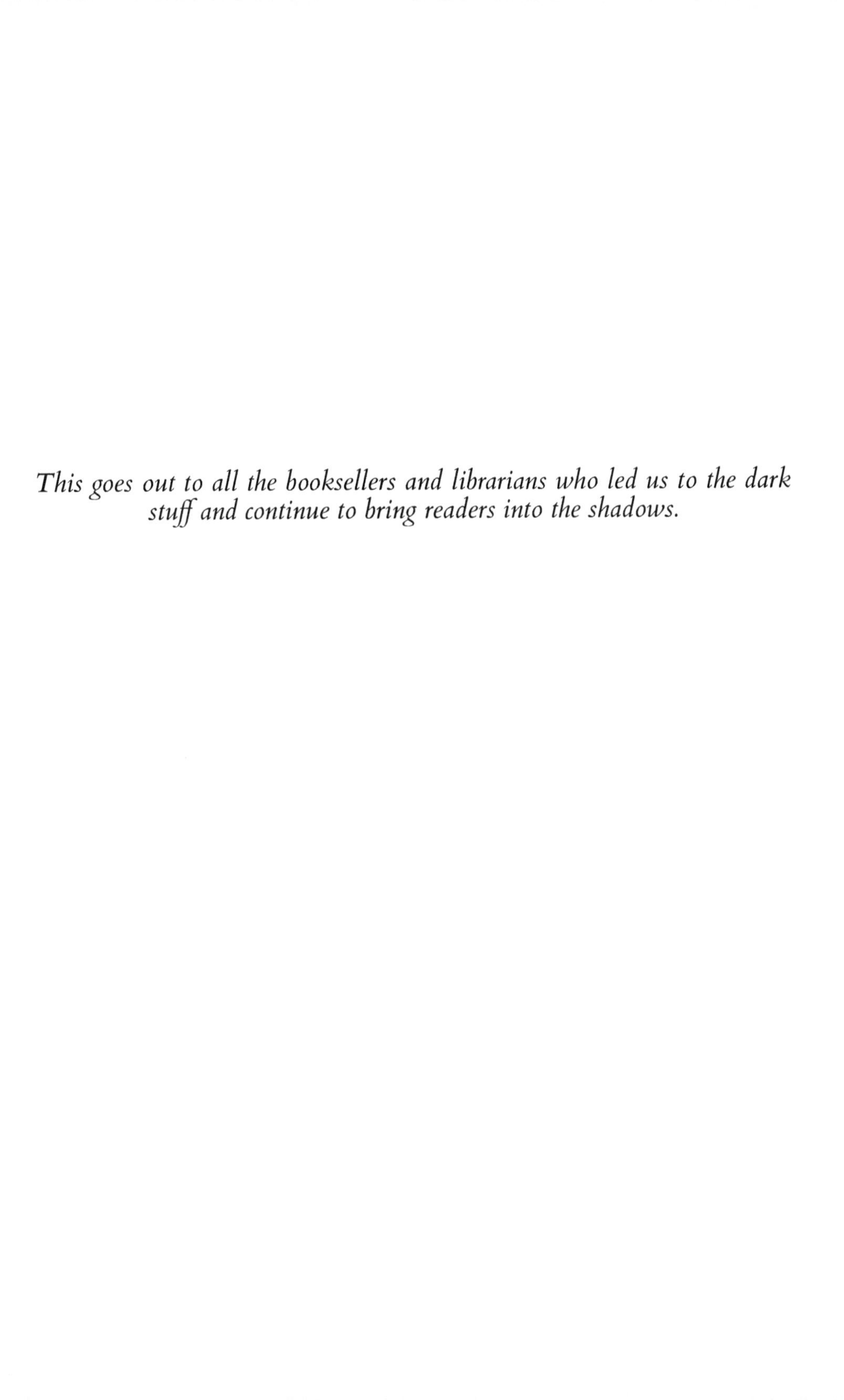

This goes out to all the booksellers and librarians who led us to the dark stuff and continue to bring readers into the shadows.

MORBIDOLOGIES

by Shane D. Keene

the handle of an
ice pick
protrudes from
a socket,
a body sat
on a sofa
one-eyed
watches
blind
the blank
tv

the trails of
red are
everything,
down the hall,
in the
sheets,
behind my
vision,
down his
cheek
I sit

watching him
being a
dead man,
while the
house sleeps
like a
corpse,
children in
their beds
forever,
grandma in
the attic
swinging,
mother in
the bath
in a state of
deepest
shock,
blue eyes
bulging,
black lips
burning,
grandpa
turning on
the spit,
plumping
flesh
charred and
split

so many ways
to die,
so many ways
to try
before the
night
declines
such a way

to be,
to embrace the
curiosities,
carve and cut,
dissect and
discern,
so many
things left
to learn,
morbidologies
to invent,
bone and
flesh
to break
and mold,
and terrors
both subliminal &
evident,
dermal layers
to part,
unfold, turn
like pages
in a wicked
tome;

read the sigils,
decipher the
forbidden,
peel the
lies away,
& yield to
what you've
hidden
from yourself.

TABLE OF CONTENTS

MORBIDOLOGIES

An Introduction

If you've written or read horror long enough, I bet you have, at some point, had some refer to you with the snooty sobriquet of *morbid.* You're *morbid* to like those kinds of stories. You're *morbid* to dwell over things gory or macabre. You're *morbid* to wonder what it would sound like to crush someone's windpipe or raise a demon within the confines of a salt circle.

You're just fucking *morbid.*

Fine…but are you? Really?

Morbidity doesn't simply mean you like something or enjoy it. You can *like* something—anything—without being morbid, whether that's creampuffs, Bea Arthur, or funeral practices. No. Morbidity layers a whole other stratum on top of that. It means you aren't just interested in or delighted with something. It means you're obsessed with it, possessed by it in a rather unhealthy kind of way.

But that's just the half of it. I mean, don't get me wrong, you *can* be obsessed with cream puffs or Bea Arthur in a thoroughly unwholesome manner, I suppose, in ways we won't touch on here but you are welcome to entertain right now all on your own. There…finished? Right, let's all bathe and move on.

Being morbid means being obsessed with disturbing or unpleasant subjects. That surely includes most of the themes horror holds most dear—death and dying and pain and fear and the unsightly splashing of bodily fluids. But as we said going into this, a simple interest in these things is not enough. It has to be a compulsion, an overwhelming drive for and about these topics. Something that borders on a mania, a drive so encompassing it pushes out all other aspects of your life.

To sum up: liking or enjoying something, not morbid. Obsessing over normal things, not morbid. Obsessing over somewhat distasteful matters. Ding-ding-ding! *Morbid.*

What makes the creator and consumer of these morbidities something less than morbid themselves? The ability to answer the question, "Why do you?" with "Because I love it."

What you hold in your hands now is a collection of such obsessions, an exemplary tome of lessons in the truly morbid, the twisted, the outright horrifying. Consider this *Morbidologies* 101.

Class begins in 3…2…

Shane D. Keene
Portland, Oregon

&

John F.D. Taff
Southern Illinois

February 2023

PLUCK

by Sonora Taylor

Marleigh closed her eyes. "Hold still," her mother said. Marleigh felt a long rip followed by a soothing burn across her forehead. Tingles sparked and crawled all over her like tiny bugs released from the forest of her eyebrows.

"Okay, let's shape them up," her mother said, holding a pair of tweezers.

Marleigh sat still through each and every pull. Pluck, pluck, pluck! A sharp but passing pain as each little bug was freed. Marleigh watched as her mother wiped the tweezers on a cotton rag draped over her knee. Single hairs stared up at her like amputated legs, curling upwards towards her face and crying out for the bodies left behind beneath her skin.

"That should give you a nice permanent shape," her mother said with a smile as she held up a mirror. "But you'll still have to pluck some hairs here and there every couple of weeks."

Marleigh stared at her newly freed skin. Her eyes had never looked so wide. She brushed a fingertip over her reddened skin. A bump cut off her path.

"The welts go away after a few hours," her mother explained.

Or after the bodies are plucked, Marleigh thought.

"We can get you some essence, if you like," her mother offered. "Something to soothe the skin."

Marleigh shook her head, then smiled as she took the tweezers from her mother's hand. From that day forward, Marleigh couldn't pass a mirror without looking for more little legs to remove.

Marleigh was used to things growing where they weren't supposed to. As a small child, she helped her mother pluck bugs from their vegetable patch and pull weeds from their flower garden. "Useless things," her mother often muttered as she held up clumps of wilted, scraggly roots from the earth.

Marleigh noticed her own hair falling in similar patterns down the side of her face. "Like this?" she asked as she held up her tresses.

"No, Marleigh, your hair isn't useless at all. Don't be stupid."

Marleigh pressed her lips together. She hated it when her words made her mother angry. Whenever she felt something stupid about to pass through her lips, she kept them closed. Whenever she thought about saying something, the words would swarm against her mouth like her mother's hated bugs. Words were bugs, and Marleigh had to keep them hidden.

"She's so quiet," her grandmother often remarked when she would come over for tea and cigarettes with Marleigh's mother.

"Better seen and not heard, right?" her mother would say, and both would chuckle and sometimes cough around the smoke coming out of their mouths.

With nowhere else to go, the bugs found other ways to wriggle their way out of Marleigh's body. She couldn't stop looking at her hair, their brown misshapen strands crawling over her face, and think of them as weeds upon which the bugs loved to feast. She twirled the roots in her fingers. One day, she pulled. The rip washed over her scalp as all the bugs fled, then stopped. It felt good.

"Marleigh, what are you doing to your hair?" her mother cried the first time she saw her do it. She swatted Marleigh's hand away. "Stop it."

Marleigh couldn't stop. "Quit yanking at your hair," her mother said when she caught her again. "Or you're going to ruin it." But Marleigh knew she couldn't ruin what was already sullied.

"Mary Leighann, that's it!" her mother huffed one day as she dragged her into the bathroom. "You hate your hair so much? Here." She held Marleigh down with one hand and pulled out an electric razor with the other. Marleigh gasped as her mother began to shave off the roots one by one.

"There," her mother said as she threw the razor onto the sink with a loud thunk. "Can't keep ruining it if you don't got it to begin with."

Marleigh ran her hand over her newly shorn scalp. The bugs tingled beneath, but she knew from experience they'd simmer down after a while. They'd find somewhere else to crawl.

"Oh Jesus." Her mother put a palm to her mouth. "Oh Christ, I'm sorry, Marleigh. I shouldn't have—"

Marleigh turned and hugged her mother. She froze, but after a moment, returned her daughter's embrace. She caressed Marleigh's head, something she almost never did.

"She looks like a little Nazi," her grandmother observed the next day over tea.

"Mama!"

"Like those skinheads you see walking around."

"Hush. She does not."

"Or like that bitch that tore up the picture of the Pope on TV. Don't know which is worse."

"She likes it. Leave her be."

Marleigh smiled as she played with her Barbies. Her head was free of roots, and she could keep it that way with the flick of a razor. The bugs were still inside, but Marleigh could keep them there, buried where her mother wouldn't see them.

Or so Marleigh thought. When she was fourteen years old, her mother suggested she pluck her eyebrows. "Just to shape them up," she said as she held Marleigh's chin. "Open up that pretty face of yours."

Marleigh didn't think it was that pretty. It looked better without the ugly roots growing out of the top, but her face was still crawling with bugs, pushing at her lips when she refused to say a word. Now they were wiggling out of her forehead. How had she never noticed them before? All their creepy little legs, lying dormant and waiting to burst out of her skin and wreak havoc.

Like the day she'd shaved her head, though, her mother saved the day. The waxing and plucking made them scurry to find new places to hide. Unlike the electric razor, which Marleigh's mother wouldn't let her use—"You can't see the back of your head, you'll mess it all up," she'd tsked—she'd been given the tweezer. Now she could take care of the bugs on her own.

It seemed, though, that the bugs grew in stubbornness each time she plucked them. She was vehement about getting each stray leg out from above her eyes, and yet more were waiting for her the next day. When she closed her eyes at night, she dreamed of thousands of mites breeding beneath her forehead, crawling and squirming until they squished together and squeezed through her skin, one at a time, wriggling and writhing.

"Don't pluck too much," her mother said one day as Marleigh sat in front of her magnified mirror. "You've got such a nice shape, no one will notice a stray hair or two."

Marleigh noticed, and Marleigh needed to do something about it. She tweezed when she could. She used her fingers when she couldn't.

"Stop picking at your face," her mother scolded at the dinner table. "You're going to get ingrown hairs."

Marleigh didn't listen. Nothing could be worse than the bugs she felt scurrying and scurrying—

"Marleigh…"

Burrowing and digging and crawling—

"Mary Leighann…"

Digging deeper and deeper into her head, but they wouldn't be able to if Marleigh could just…get…their…legs—

Crack!

Marleigh jumped at the sound of her mother's knife slamming against her plate. Her mother leapt from her seat and yanked Marleigh's hand away from her face.

"Stop it!" Marleigh shrieked.

She snapped her mouth shut, curled her tongue back and pursed her lips. But it was too late. Her mother smacked her across her cheek. "Don't you dare speak for the first time in years just to sass me!" she yelled. "And if you keep picking at your eyebrows like that, you're going to be bald all over your goddamn face."

Marleigh ignored her. Her focus stayed on the stinging burn across her cheek.

Her mother huffed as she grabbed Marleigh's plate, still half full of food. "You never say a word, you just keep picking at the hairs on your head like a fucking freak," she snapped as she chucked the plate into the sink.

The stinging cooled into a tingle, just like it'd done when her mother waxed her eyebrows. The bugs had moved.

"And when you do talk, it's to disrespect me. You know how much I put up with for you?"

The bugs were near her mouth.

"I lost my figure, my boyfriend, all for you. I lost my time. I lost my *life*." She pointed a finger at Marleigh, who continued to stare into space deep in thought. "And for that I get you, who can't stop plucking her eyebrows, pulling her hair…"

The bugs were *in* her mouth.

"…or only speaking up to talk *back* to me!"

There was only one bug. A big, giant worm that all the other bugs were trying to escape from.

"That goddamn tongue of yours. I don't know where you got it from, but it sure as hell didn't come from me."

The worm that made her mother angry in the garden. The worm that made her angry now.

The worm that both she and her grandmother preferred to lay limp and dormant.

"If you don't get your act together soon, I'm going to—"

Her mother froze as Marleigh grabbed the knife from her plate. Marleigh closed her eyes and pulled out her tongue, holding it taut.

"Marleigh!" her mother shrieked. But all Marleigh could feel was a worm wriggling in her fingers—one that would stop the moment it was plucked.

THE THIRD SHANNON

by Jonathan Janz

Please, he thought. *Please understand.*

She won't, the skeptic in him argued. *They never do. How many have you brought in here?*

Doesn't matter, he argued.

Twelve? Thirteen?

They weren't special enough. They weren't Tabitha.

Tabitha closed her eyes and extended her arms. "I'm afraid I'm gonna run into something."

"Trust," Eric reminded her.

His hands on her shoulders, Eric guided her toward the green door. He preferred blindfolds, but Tabitha was claustrophobic and he didn't want that spoiling the surprise.

"Stand still a second," he told her.

When he reached into his pocket he heard her gasp. She'd opened her eyes.

"Hey!" he shouted.

But she was bouncing on her heels and smiling her adorable smile. "I get to enter the forbidden room?"

He affected a crooked grin. "A six-month anniversary should be special, right?"

She rubbed her hands together. "Best gift ever."

He chuckled softly. "Alright. Close your eyes. For real this time."

Tabitha obliged, though she was still smiling. He fitted the key in the lock, twisted the knob, checked to make sure her eyes were shut, and opened the green door. The familiar charge surged through him. He wondered if Tabitha could feel it pulse through his fingers as he guided her inside.

"Okay," he said.

She opened her eyes. Breath held, he watched her face. There wasn't the wonder he'd hoped to see, but neither was there the horror or disgust he'd beheld on too many occasions.

"First impressions?" he asked.

"Is this your theater room?"

"Sure, it's that. But take a minute to look around. Drink it all in."

As she did, Eric tried to view the room through her eyes. The black leather recliners angled toward the flatscreen. The surround sound speakers expertly positioned for maximum auditory immersion. The posters he'd not only framed, but equipped with colored LED borders, which he'd currently switched to fuchsia because it was more erotic.

Tabitha gazed at a poster. Did she see it for the work of art it was? No longer able to control himself, he sidled up to her.

"*Scorned*," he explained. "One of Shannon Tweed's best films."

Tabitha studied the poster a moment longer, then drifted to the next.

He kept his voice casual. "*Mirror Images II,* starring Shannon Whirry. A classic."

This time she didn't pause but graduated to the next poster. Eric felt his smile falter but reminded himself to be patient. Tabitha was different. She had to be.

He tapped the glossy poster frame. "*Play Time.* Monique Parent and Jennifer Burton. A bona fide masterpiece."

She nodded absently and stepped to the center of the room.

"So?" he said.

She chewed her lip. "You're into porn?"

He winced, his insides plummeting. He took a moment to compose himself. *Give her time. It's a lot to take in.*

She's like all the others, the skeptic declared. *Judgmental and frigid.*

He conjured what he hoped was an easy smile. "No, Tabitha, I'm not into porn."

Her eyes shifted to the poster for *Body Chemistry 4: Full Exposure.*

He laughed, but it sounded high and forced, the titter of a guilty child. "Don't be misled by titles. That's a common mistake."

She looked at him dubiously.

He explained, "Hardcore pornography is just—and please forgive my directness—but it's just fucking. It's putting two people, or three, or ten, in a room and ordering them to go at it." He backpedaled to the poster beside the flatscreen. "Now take this one. *Sins of Desire.* You know who starred in it? Tanya Roberts."

No recognition in her face.

"*Tanya-freaking-Roberts,*" he said. When she only shrugged apologetically, he gestured at the poster, which featured Tanya in a sheer sable body suit. "We're talking about a mainstream actress here. She was in *The Beastmaster. Sheena.* Hell, she was the title character." He hurried toward Tabitha. "Don't you see? A respected artist like Tanya Roberts would never have degraded herself with hardcore porn." He flourished a hand. "Softcore is the antithesis of that. Softcore is transcendent."

"Don't people have sex in them?"

He sighed. "I'm not explaining myself clearly. Why don't you have a seat, and I'll take you through it."

"I'd prefer to stand," she answered.

Ah fuck, he thought.

But he clenched his teeth against the wave of desperation. "Listen, softcore isn't what you think. There's no exploitation in these films. No bodily fluids spurting all over people's faces. This is tasteful, with high production value. The people who made these movies actually cared about story. About beauty. The sex is simulated, but the passion is real."

Tabitha exhaled, her cheeks puffing out. "I guess everyone has their kinks. It's not one I've heard before, but…I like you, Eric." She tilted her head. "Does this have something to do with why you won't…you know…"

Febrile tension encircled his neck, the room suddenly twenty degrees too warm. She edged closer and Eric overmastered an insane urge to run. No woman had ever stayed this long without fleeing or branding him a creep, but now that he'd ventured this far he had no idea how to proceed.

A voice in his head spoke up: *Tell her the rest.*

Eric's throat went dry. *I can't.*

Yet Tabitha's eyes were compassionate. He thought of the many times they'd made out, the kittenish moans she'd emitted as he stroked her through her clothes. And even though she'd seen the room, she hadn't fled. Maybe she truly was the one.

Tell her, the voice persisted.

"Eric?" she said, her voice gentle. "Talk to me?"

He swallowed. "Okay. I'll tell you. But first…will you please sit?"

This time she didn't argue.

He crossed to the faux-mahogany cabinet where he kept his collection, selected the proper key, and unlocked it. He bypassed the DVDs and retrieved a plain white VHS cassette holder, as well as a plump manilla folder bound together with sturdy black clips. He knelt before Tabitha and placed the white VHS case in her lap. Two words had been scrawled on the case in blue marker.

"*Illicit Images*," she read.

He waited.

"Is it a movie?"

He nodded.

She frowned at the case. "Do…you want to watch it?"

"Open it," he said.

She did. It was empty.

She cocked an eyebrow at him.

"This," he said, tapping the inside of the case, "is the Holy Grail of softcore."

"I don't understand."

"When I was a kid, I was obsessed with Cinemax. Late-night Cinemax."

A smile tugged at her lips. "You mean Skinemax?"

He laughed, and she did too. It rallied his spirits. "That's what my friends called it, too. I haven't told you much about my childhood—"

"You haven't told me anything."

"I know. My mom left when I was little. My dad, he was also into late-night Cinemax. I'd have it on in my bedroom, and when I'd mute my TV I'd hear it in the living room too."

"You and your dad bonded over porn?"

"*It's not porn!*"

Tabitha recoiled.

He forced his hands to unclench. She'd seen it though. Her gaze was fearful again.

You've failed, he thought. *You've failed and now you'll have to spend the rest of your savings on what's probably a dead end.*

No! he thought.

He took a steadying breath. "One afternoon I came home after school and saw this." He indicated the case. "We never talked about it, but I knew Dad was into softcore, and he knew that I knew." Eric leaned forward. "But this case was empty."

She lowered her chin. "Did you find another copy?"

"That's just it. There is no other copy. Not a single copy in existence. When I asked Dad about it, he claimed he had no idea where the case came from."

"So it's a fake?"

He sprang to his feet. "No! It isn't. It's real. Look…" He retrieved the manila folder and unclipped it. "Here's the IMDB listing."

"IMDB?"

"Internet Movie Database." He turned the page. "And here's a fragment of the screenplay. *The climactic scene.*"

"Aren't there a lot of screenplays that don't get made into movies?"

He was already nodding. "Yes, but the IMDB entry suggests it's real." He flipped to the last paper in the folder. "And there's this."

Tabitha squinted. "Who is that?"

"That," he said solemnly, "is the third Shannon."

She squinted at him. "Third Shannon?"

He scurried to the *Scorned* poster. "This is Shannon Tweed. Softcore goddess. Wife of KISS bassist Gene Simmons."

Tabitha didn't answer.

He crossed to *Mirror Images II* and tapped the protective plastic. "Shannon Whirry. Another legend. I can't tell you how many nights I've spent watching her."

He resumed his place at Tabitha's feet, nodded at the black-and-white printout she held. "And that's Shannon Vale. The third Shannon."

"Is she as famous as the others?"

"That's just it. She only made one movie."

"*Illicit Images*?"

"Yes! So you see why I need to solve the mystery?"

"Is the film worth a lot of money?"

"I'm sure it is, but this isn't about money." He tapped the paper. "That's a screencap from the movie. Look at Shannon Vale. Really look at her."

They were silent a moment.

"Okay?" Tabitha said.

"She's breathtaking, right?"

"I suppose…"

"And this," he riffled through the screenplay, "is the most erotic scene I've ever read." His eyes fell on a passage, and like always, it drew him in. He began to perspire.

"Eric?"

He shook himself free. "Sorry. I just…"

She closed the folder. "Eric, I can see this is important to you…"

His stomach began to sink.

"…but I can't understand what this has to do with our sex life."

He moved away from her and braced a hand on the wall. "You're right. You've been patient. You've been…more understanding than the others."

"Others?"

"I need to be truthful with you," he hastened on. "I have to come clean."

Eric turned and faced Tabitha, who looked very small in the recliner.

"Tabitha, I'm haunted."

"Haunted," she repeated. "Like, by a ghost?"

"In a way, yes. Ever since I started researching Shannon Vale, back when I was a teenager, I, um…haven't been able to perform."

"You mean you've never had sex?"

"Not with a partner."

The ripple of disgust on her face was unmistakable.

"I haven't been able to," he admitted. "When I'm alone, with my starlets, everything is fine. More than fine. But when I'm with an actual woman…it's not the same." He took a step toward her. "But I'll be able to with you. All you've got to do is…"

Her voice was as cold as her eyes. "Is what?"

He ventured a smile. "Act out the scene with me?"

He expected her to bolt from the room. To rip the folder in half.

Instead, she thumbed through the pages. "Fine," she said.

He gaped at her. "Seriously?"

"If that's what it takes, sure. I care about you, Eric. And I've been dying to sleep with you since our first date."

He knew how dopey his grin must be, but he didn't give a damn. "Okay. Let's get ready."

"Get ready?"

"Yes!" he laughed as he hurried toward the door. "We've gotta get our costumes on!"

It was a disaster.

The problems started with wardrobe. *Illicit Images* centered on Shannon Vale's character, a high-powered defense attorney who develops an attraction for the man she's representing in a murder case. The actor who played him—also the director of the film—was

Kevin Reeves, who'd appeared in several softcore classics, and not only was the man's name eerily like his own, Eric Reed, but the two of them shared a passing resemblance. A coincidence to be sure, but there were too many coincidences for his obsession to be anything but fate.

Yet when Tabitha entered his bedroom, her green dress wasn't snug like it was supposed to be.

"What's wrong?" she asked.

He leaned back on the bed. "The screenplay talks about cleavage."

"So?"

"So it's in all caps—CLEAVAGE."

She crossed her arms. "I can't help it. The dress is two sizes too big for me."

"Can't you push them up a little?"

She blew a lock of hair out of her eyes. "I'm feeling a little insulted."

He went to her and put his hands on her shoulders. "Don't be like that."

She gave him a look.

"Come on," he said, returning to the bed. "The handcuffs are on the nightstand."

Tabitha scooped up the cuffs. "You're sure you want to wear these?"

He raised his arms above his head. "That's the whole point of the scene. Shannon Vale's character is supposed to turn the tables on her lover. She's supposed to dominate him."

"Mm," Tabitha said, climbing onto the bed. "I like that." She fastened a cuff around his wrist, then breathed into his ear. "You want me to dominate you?"

"Use the screenplay," he directed.

She favored him with a wry smile, fed the short chain through the spindly headboard he'd special-ordered, then clicked the second cuff on his wrist. She plucked the screenplay from the bed. "Oooh. It says I'm supposed to mount you."

His breathing had gone shallow. "Don't say what's in it. Just act it out."

Tabitha placed the pages on the bed beside him and straddled him. Her eyes on the screenplay, she read, "'You've been a naughty boy.'"

An unaccustomed tingle kindled in Eric's loins.

She must have noticed because she ground her buttocks into him. "'I think you need punished.'"

"'Need *to be* punished,'" he corrected.

"Huh?"

"The script says 'You need *to be* punished,' not 'You need punished.'"

"*Okaaay*," she answered.

He fought off a surge of annoyance.

She glanced at the script. "It says I hitch up—sorry. Forgot I'm not supposed to narrate." She rucked the green dress up her thighs, but the tingle had begun to recede.

She read, "'The judge and jury might not have punished you, but I—'" She broke off, made a coughing sound, and he realized she was stifling laughter. She cleared her throat. "'But I will show you what happens to bad little boys.'" She lowered herself onto him and kissed his neck, but her body shook with barely restrained giggles.

He scowled at the ceiling. "Tabitha…"

"It's Shannon," she breathed and nibbled his earlobe. "Oh—sorry. That's the actress. My character name is Jasmine." She was shaking harder. "Jasmine Cozumel."

"Dammit, Tabitha!"

"I'm trying," she said, breathless now. "It's just...I'm sorry. It says I'm supposed to lick your nipple."

"Undo the cuffs."

"Eric—"

"Undo the goddamned cuffs!"

She unlocked him. When he pushed off the bed and stalked from the room, she scampered after him. "I was doing my best. It's not easy to read those lines—"

"The problem wasn't the lines." He jerked on his robe and shouldered past her toward the living room. "The problem is you."

"Eric, you don't have to get mad."

"You're like all the others," he snapped. "You have no respect for art."

"*Art?* Jesus, it's just porn without the good stuff."

"Get out."

"You act like Tanya Rogers—"

"*Roberts.*"

"—is some fucking Oscar winner." She stormed over and retrieved her clothes. "And how many fucking Shannons can there be?"

"Shut up."

"Hurt your feelings did I? Talked bad about your girlfriend?"

"You need to stop."

She cocked a hip and tossed her hair. "The beguiling Shannon Vale?"

"Tabitha..."

"She doesn't even exist."

"*Watch your fucking mouth!*"

She froze. Her eyes were very wide, very afraid. Wordlessly, she scurried to the door, fumbled with the lock, then wrested it open and slipped through.

Eric stood there, his heart slamming. "She does exist," he murmured. "She *does* exist."

He locked the door, snagged his laptop from the couch, and logged into the forum. After some searching, he found the user he was looking for. He clicked *ratlover221*, chose MESSAGE, and typed, "The McDonald's on Church St. Tomorrow at noon. I'll bring the money. No bullshit."

He hit SEND and snapped the laptop shut. It was most of his savings, but it would be worth it. It had to be. He'd been a fool to think just any woman could capture the magic of Shannon Vale.

The only solution was finding the real thing.

At half-past-noon the man in the olive-colored jacket slid into the booth. The guy had a deep tan and a sooty growth of beard. His head was nearly-shaved, but what was left of his prickly black hair was receding. They regarded each other in silence.

"You have something for me?" the man asked. He sounded like he had laryngitis.

Eric studied him. "You Rat Lover?"

The man looked away. "I don't know who that is." He had an accent, maybe French, and though he didn't look much like a rat, he did resemble some other small animal. A ferret maybe. "You bring the money?"

"The info first," Eric answered.

Rat Lover's eyes swung up. He uttered a soft laugh. "No way. I give you the information, you leave without giving me money."

Eric eyed him a long moment, then reached into his khaki trousers. Rat Lover's eyes widened when he beheld the plump envelope.

"If you fuck me over," Eric said, "I will hunt you down and beat you to death."

Rat Lover shrugged. "You're in good shape. But you'll never find me."

Eric slid toward the edge of the booth.

"Wait," Rat Lover said and extended a palm. Eric only paused a moment before relinquishing the envelope. Rat Lover opened it and peered inside. "It's all here?"

"Fifteen thousand."

Rat Lover licked his lips. "You really must have it bad."

"Tell me."

Rat Lover seemed to think it over. Then he stashed the envelope in an inner pocket of his jacket and sat forward. "She is living in El Segundo with her husband. You will find her at this address." He slid a folded scrap of paper across the table.

Eric took it. "You're sure it's her."

"Of course I am. I would not accept your money otherwise."

"If it's not…"

"You have my word."

Eric watched him a long beat. Then he rose and made to leave.

Rat Lover's hand clamped over his wrist. "You realize she might not even come to the door. This husband of hers…my source says he's dangerous. My source claims this husband is the reason she hasn't acted since the one movie."

Eric stared down at Rat Lover and decided the man was telling the truth. "Have you seen it? *Illicit Images*?"

Rat Lover grinned. "You know the answer, my friend. *No one* has seen it. This husband of hers, he is consumed with jealousy. He was so angry at the men she appeared with in the film—and the one woman—that he destroyed all the copies."

"But how could he do that? Was her husband the producer or something?"

"Producer?" Rat Lover said. "My friend, he was the producer, the director, the screenwriter, and the star. The famous Eric Reeves."

The drive to El Segundo only took an hour, but locating the property proved difficult. When he fed the address Rat Lover provided into his phone, he ended up at a vacant lot. He got out and looked around, but the only house in the area was a quarter-mile distant, and it was so tucked away in a fig grove that he would have missed it entirely if not for the wheel ruts that cut through the sloping scrub brush.

Eric took a chance and followed the path. He carried with him a briefcase he hoped looked official. But as he neared the scarlet front door, uncertainty took hold and refused to be displaced. For one thing, the house was single-storied and far too sleek, the front of it all windows. Though the *Illicit Images* screenplay didn't describe the house, Eric had always imagined it as a sprawling mansion. This resembled some sort of Zen garden where one might meditate rather than stage the climax of a steamy noir film.

He compelled himself toward the scarlet door. He'd come too far and spent too much money to merely turn tail and return to his sad apartment. He knocked and fought the urge to bolt. This was all a mistake. Shannon Vale didn't live here. And if she did, it would be her husband or a servant who'd open the door. To his knowledge no one had seen Shannon since the movie had been shot. What made him believe she'd suddenly materialize for him?

A soft clunk made him stand ramrod straight. Someone turning a lock. The door creaked open.

It was Shannon Vale.

Eric forgot to breathe.

She was older, of course, probably fifty, but she was more beautiful than he could have imagined. Her hair was long, dark, wavy. She still had the beguiling bangs she'd favored in his lone picture of her. Her eyes were a dazzling brown, and her heart-shaped chin tapered so endearingly that he wanted to cry. She wore a robe, a burgundy robe, and it was this that undid him, that brought the truth avalanching down on him: Shannon was real. Achingly real. She was every bit as ethereal as he'd dreamed her to be.

And that was why he had to leave. To her he was a random man, a stalker who'd paid to locate her whereabouts. As if to confirm this, she cinched the edges of her robe tighter and watched him with those profound eyes. *He'd* put that fear into them. *He'd* disquieted this enchanting, mystical creature.

"I'm sorry," he said and took a backward step. "I think I have the wrong place." His voice sounded froggy and pathetic. He turned to flee. What a disaster. His life had crescendoed to this moment and he couldn't have botched it any worse.

"Are you here to see me?" she called.

His back to her, he froze.

"Did you maybe," she went on, "come to give me something?"

His limbs went slack. He swallowed. Turned to face her. "Give you something?"

She nodded, and now…was there a plea in her eyes?

Last chance, he thought. *If you don't take it you might as well be dead.*

He drew in what breath he could. Reciting the screenplay fragment he knew by heart, he said, "I came to give you your heart's desire."

Her eyes absolutely blazed. Not with outrage, not with contempt. With passion. With hope.

A corner of her mouth rose. "Then why don't you come inside and give it to me?"

The dining room wasn't as he'd pictured it, but somehow it was right. It had a timeless style, one he could imagine as the setting for the pivotal *Illicit Images* dinner scene. Lengthy, a bit narrow, teak-floored. Three walls of burnished wood with inset shelves housing various knickknacks, the other wall comprised of enormous panes of glass opening onto a lush courtyard. As Shannon led him into the room, he could hear a fountain burbling. It soothed his jangled nerves, made him forget about the briefcase banging against his leg as Shannon ushered him to his seat.

"'Bet you never thought you'd see the inside of my home,'" she recited.

My God, he thought. She not only uttered the scripted words verbatim, her delivery was sublime. An actress this talented should've had a long, illustrious career.

He had to elevate his game to match hers. Eric took a moment to recall the exact screenplay wording.

"'It sure as hell beats Tannenworth,'" he said, referring to the fictitious prison from which her character, Defense Attorney Jasmine Cozumel, springs him despite his guilt.

She gave him a come-hither smirk. "'And do you like what you see here?'"

"'Big time,'" he answered, giving it just the right hint of innuendo. His character, Brock Coghlan, was a man of few words.

"'Dinner will be ready soon,'" she said. "'I need fresh clothing on my skin.'"

He waited until she was nearly to the doorway before calling, "'But not too much clothing, eh?'"

She smoldered at him over her shoulder, and the heat in her eyes made him grasp the edge of his chair for support. She vamped away. Eric waited a few seconds, then pumped a fist. *Jesus*. Never in his wildest dreams would he have guessed it would go this well. To burn off some nervous energy, he moved about the room, examined the various figurines and curios nested in the cubbies. He was turning over an emerald-green bowl, which was weighty and sheened with a glittery glaze, when a deep male voice made him jump and damn near drop it.

"Shannon tells me you're an old friend."

Eric stared at the man in the doorway. It was Eric Reeves, of that there was no doubt. Unlike his younger wife, time had ravaged this man. His hair, once so lustrous and brown, had faded to winter white. His muscles seemed to have deflated and pooled around his waist. His clothes bespoke of conservative affluence, pressed gray slacks and a crisp pink dress shirt. Reeves had been a fixture of nineties' softcore and had accrued so much cachet that he'd founded his own production company. He wondered if Reeves would notice how he'd modeled his entire look on him. Or Reeves as he'd been in his prime—the deeply-tanned stud—not the paunchy investment banker he now resembled.

Reeves stepped nearer and waved his arms as though Eric were in a trance. "Hellooo? Earth to stranger?"

"Sorry," Eric muttered and gestured vaguely. "'This is a fine place you've got.'"

Yes, he thought. *Stick to the script. Even if this jerkwad doesn't.*

Reeves nodded. "It's home. You got a name?"

No going back now. He extended a hand. "'Brock Coghlan.'"

Reeves's eyes narrowed. "Coghlan, huh?"

The moment drew out. Just when Eric was sure Reeves would

bust him and send him packing or call the police, he seized Eric's hand and pumped it twice. A strong grip.

But a feeble mind. My God, Reeves hadn't even recognized the words that he himself had written! In his defense, *Illicit Images* had been made a quarter-century ago and never released, but Eric still judged it pretty incredible Reeves didn't remember his own screenplay.

Shannon reentered, and Eric had to sit to keep from swooning. She'd donned a green dress, and even though the screenplay had simply read SNUG GREEN DRESS ACCENTUATING HER CURVES, he knew this was the same dress she'd sported in *Illicit Images*. It had to be.

The table was fifteen feet long. Reeves took his place at the head directly opposite Eric. Shannon brought the men glasses of water and sat equidistant from them, the courtyard to her back.

"The quiche will be ready soon," she told them.

Reeves grunted. "Quiche? Whatever happened to a good old-fashioned steak, am I right?"

Eric arranged his features into commiseration. Brock Coghlan was a brutish man with boundless animal magnetism, but he knew when to play nice. It was necessary to lead the husband on for their plot to work.

"Back where I'm from," Eric improvised, "they can't spell 'quiche,' much less eat it."

Reeves roared laughter. Shannon fixed Eric with a hungry gaze.

Reeves wiped his eyes. "So where you from, Coghlan?"

Eric resisted an urge to look at Shannon. Reeves had asked the exact thing the husband asked in the screenplay—he was quoting himself without realizing it!

"'I'm from around,'" Eric answered. "'You know, here and there.'"

Reeves's smile vanished. "No really. Where are you from?"

Eric sat up straighter. "Reseda."

Reeves's eyes narrowed. "So you're not in the industry?"

Eric glanced at Shannon, whose features had tightened. He didn't like going off-script. Not only was there no fun in it, he could fuck up royally and wreck the whole plan.

"The reason I ask," Reeves went on, "is your briefcase. Being a producer, I meet a lot of desperate people." He eyeballed Eric. "You're not one of them, are you?"

Eric shook his head and attempted a smile.

"Then what's in the briefcase?" Reeves persisted.

Just when he was certain he'd have to open the briefcase and reveal its contents, a *ding* sounded from the kitchen.

"The quiche!" Shannon cried. With a nervous smile, she bustled from the dining room.

But Reeves continued to study him in that piercing way of his. "You know, we get crazies out here from time to time."

"You don't say?"

A closed-eyed nod. "I'm very protective of Shannon. That's why I rescued her from the scene."

Eric sipped his water. "The scene?"

"Erotica," Reeves explained. "You're no doubt aware of my profession?"

Eric shrugged. "I might have seen a couple films."

Reeves chuckled, his belly jiggling. "Might have seen a couple… my friend, who do you think you're fooling? I can see it all over you."

Eric coughed. "Excuse me?"

"You're a *fan*," Reeves said, spreading his arms. "I mean, just look at you. Dark, handsome, you got the muscles. The hair." He narrowed his eyes and wagged an index finger. "In fact, you remind me of myself, back when I was in front of the camera."

No use pretending. "You got me. I'm a fan."

Reeves slapped the table and laughed, their water glasses jouncing. "I knew it. I just knew it." He leaned forward. "So what's your favorite movie of mine? *Carnal Intrigue*? *Uma's Urges*? No, wait. *Hollywood Temptations*. Everybody digs that one."

Eric took a long drag of water and wiped his lips. "Actually, my tastes are a bit more esoteric. *Illicit Images*?"

All mirth bled from Reeves's face. "My God. You're one of those."

Shannon entered bearing three plates, but she stopped when she discovered the two men staring at each other. "What's wrong?"

Reeves jabbed a finger at Eric. "He's one of them. I knew it the first time I laid eyes on him."

Shannon's hands trembled as she settled the plates on the table. "Honey, I'm sure Mr. Coghlan means no harm."

"Bullshit," Reeves snapped. "I know his type. I've seen 'em sneak onto sets, pretend they're part of the crew—"

"Honey—"

"—just to see some tits! On the set of *Kama Sutra Nights* some nutjob tried to bust into Mia Zottoli's trailer. God knows what might've happened if we hadn't caught him."

Shannon placed a conciliatory hand on her husband's shoulder, but Reeves shrugged it off. "You don't get it, baby. This is exactly the sort of shit I rescued you from. Weirdos, creeps. They act innocent, but they're worse than the hardcore porn addicts. Guys like these, they're so maladjusted they can't stand the thought of their starlets having actual sex with other people."

Shannon's expression was pained. "Darling, let's just turn down the temperature, okay? I'm sure Mr. Coghlan is harmless."

"Harmless?" Reeves demanded. "He wants you for himself! That's the whole point of softcore. These fucking psychos believe the actresses are theirs. They live in an alternate reality."

Eric sat listening to the diatribe and understood his life had been building to this moment. He retrieved the briefcase and laid it on the table before him. "You weren't saving Shannon from other men," Eric said. "You were keeping her for yourself."

Reeves rose, his jowls quivering. "Get the fuck out of my house."

Eric hesitated. But Shannon, he noticed, was edging toward him, her hands clutched to her chest. Moving deliberately, Eric got to his feet and opened the clasps of the briefcase.

Reeves didn't seem to notice; his eyes were on his wife. "What are you doing, baby?"

Shannon drifted closer to Eric.

"Baby?" Reeves called.

Eric reached into the briefcase and came out with the gun.

Reeves stood straighter. "What're you doing with that?"

"'You don't deserve Jasmine,'" Eric recited. "'She's too much woman for you.'"

"*Jasmine?*" Reeves demanded. "Who the fuck's Jasmine?"

But Eric remained in character. "'Jasmine got me acquitted from death row. She saved my life. And now I'm gonna save hers.'"

Reeves blinked at him. "You're crazy."

Shannon was beaming at Eric now.

"'This is for all the times you knocked her around,'" Eric said and raised the gun. He tried to keep the muzzle steady, but it shook wildly.

Reeves brought up his hands. "I never touched her. Baby, tell this psycho I never touched you."

Shannon gave her husband a wintry smile. "'You brought this on yourself, dear. I was supposed to be your wife, not your prisoner.'"

"*Prisoner?* What the blue fuck are you talking about?"

"'Say goodbye, you son of a bitch,'" Eric said, and squeezed the trigger.

The explosion was deafening, and they all three jumped as the wooden paneling splintered over Reeves's shoulder.

For a moment no one moved.

Reeves gaped at him. "You shot at me."

A wet heat arose in Eric's chest. Bile elevatored up his throat.

"I'm callin' the cops," Reeves muttered and pivoted toward the doorway.

"Shoot him," Shannon said.

Reeves glanced back at her, wide-eyed.

"Shoot him!" she commanded.

Eric swung the gun up and fired. He missed again, another wooden panel bursting.

Reeves spun, got tangled with a chair, and reeled across the room. Eric squeezed the trigger, but with Reeves stumbling he missed again. Reeves crashed into the wall and the emerald bowl tumbled out of its nook and shattered on the teak floor. Reeves wheeled away, but Eric stalked toward him and fired three more shots. The first shot went wide, but a pair of scarlet stains bloomed in Reeves's pink shirt, one on a shoulder blade, the other in his left side just above the belt. Reeves staggered, went down, and Eric took aim. But when he squeezed the trigger, the gun clicked empty.

"*Ah Jesus,*" Reeves groaned. "*Ah Jesus.*"

He belly-crawled, his wounds glistening in the mellow apricot light. Eric glanced at Shannon, who glowered down at her husband without pity. Both of them strode after Reeves, who left a bloody contrail behind him like some gargantuan wounded snail.

"Kill him," Shannon said.

"I'm out of bullets."

"Use the glass."

He looked blankly at her. "The glass?"

She compressed her lips, plucked the largest shard of shattered bowl from floor, and placed it in his hand. He stared down at it, appalled. Then, because he knew he'd lose what vestiges of courage he still possessed if he dallied any longer, he dropped down and sat astraddle Reeves's back. He seized the man's shock of white hair with one hand, and with the other he dragged the jagged shard of glass under the man's throat. Reeves uttered a gargling whimper, and blood drizzled over Eric's knuckles. Gasping, he jerked away and stood.

"I killed him," he whispered. "I fucking killed him."

Shannon was at his side. "Eric?"

"It was supposed to be one shot. One shot to the heart."

"There's only one scene we need to get right," she soothed. "The only one that matters."

Eric licked his lips. "We have to get rid of the body."

"Not yet," she answered. She took his hand. "First, we need to celebrate."

Her bedroom was exactly as he'd imagined it, save one detail. Rather than the wire-railed headboard the script described, the bed was a four-poster. She noticed his bemusement and said, "Remember that a movie is made three times. Once in the screenplay, once on set, and again in the editing room."

"Huh?"

"'Lay down, Brock,'" she recited.

He obeyed.

With exquisite, excruciating sensuality, she removed his clothing. Then, she fished a quartet of manacles from under the bed. These she fastened to his wrists and ankles, the extra-long chains allowing her to affix the corresponding ends to the bedposts. He could scarcely move his limbs, yet far from alarming him, this vulnerability exhilarated him. He'd never trusted someone so much in his life. And he'd never been so aroused.

Shannon went out, and when she reentered, she had fully transformed into Jasmine Cozumel. It was a subtle difference, one only a seasoned film connoisseur would detect, but the fluidity of her shoulders, the sultriness of her gaze, and the pouty set of her mouth…Jasmine was the quintessential femme fatale.

She crawled onto the bed. Like a green-dressed succubus, she mounted him.

"'You've been a naughty boy,'" she murmured.

Jesus Christ, Eric thought. *Jesus Christ.*

"'And you need to be punished.'"

Molten waves undulated through him, his erection so tumid it throbbed.

She tugged the dress up her thighs and breathed into his ear, "'The judge and jury might not have punished you, but I'm gonna show you what happens to bad little boys.'"

Eric grew lightheaded. Never in his life had he imagined pleasure like this. Her hot tongue flicked his earlobe, and she lowered herself onto him. But rather than the wet warmth he expected to feel, there was only a chilly hardness between her legs.

Eric raised his head and discovered a flesh-colored piece of curved plastic covering her sex.

"Genital guard," she explained. "We always wear them during love scenes. This one's a special model. I designed it myself."

He frowned at her.

"Oh!" she cried, her grin broadening. "I almost forgot." She leaned over him, her cleavage bulging in his face, and retrieved something from the nightstand. She scooted down his body and slipped something over his erect member that resembled a peach-hued sock. "Almost forgot yours," she said.

She resumed her position and began to writhe against him.

Bewildered, he tried to concentrate on the silk of her thighs, the dizzying sensation of her clothed breasts against his pecs, but the plastic cup over her crotch and the goddamned sock on his dick kept intruding.

"'Such a bad boy,'" she moaned, grinding harder. "'Such a nasty, guilty boy.'"

He realized her words were the last ones of the screenplay. When she paused, he was sure they were finished. She lay atop him, her voluptuous body more provocative than it had been in his fantasies.

"That's the end, right?" he asked. "The movie's over?"

Because if it is, he thought, *we can rid ourselves of these absurd impediments and experience the real thing.*

"One more page," she whispered.

He stared up at her.

"The screenplay has one more page," she told him. "An ending no one has ever seen."

His thoughts swirled. "Does Jasmine…do you…take off your clothes on the last page?"

Soft laughter. "Maybe. But there's a twist."

"A twist?"

Her heavenly face hovered over his. "The murders for which Brock Coghlan was tried? The ones of which Jasmine Cozumel got him acquitted?"

"Yeah?"

She drew something from the bodice of her dress. An icepick.

"What the hell is that?" he asked.

"'Jasmine climbs off the bed,'" she recited. She slid off him. "'She shimmies out of her dress.'" Shannon peeled the dress down her hips. Her panties and brassiere were black lace. He glimpsed her nipples and pubic hair through the fabric. Eric felt drool trickle from his mouth, but since his hands were bound, he couldn't wipe it away.

"'She fits the murder weapon into place,'" Shannon said. She snapped the wooden handle into a cylindrical slot in her genital guard so the silver point of the icepick jutted up like a needle-thin phallus.

Eric's heart began to thunder.

"There's a reason *Illicit Images* was never released," she said, crawling onto him.

"Shannon," he croaked, "whatever it is that happens in the movie—"

"In softcore," she explained, "you're not allowed to show penetration."

"Shannon, please…"

"But in this movie, we do."

He began to weep. "Shannon—"

"My name," she interrupted, "is Jasmine."

"You don't have to do this! You can just let me go!"

"Scream for me," she whispered.

"*Please!*"

Shannon raised her hips. "*Scream for me*," she moaned.

And when the ice pick punctured his perineum, Eric screamed for her.

BEYOND THE RED DOOR

by Craig Wallwork

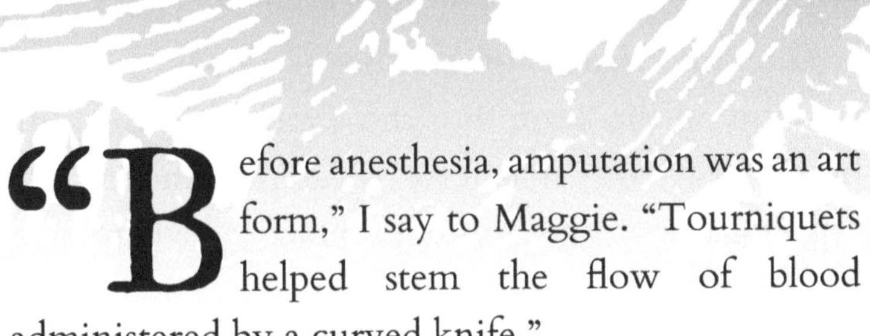

“Before anesthesia, amputation was an art form,” I say to Maggie. “Tourniquets helped stem the flow of blood administered by a curved knife.”

Tuesday is steak night. Maggie and I are sitting at the kitchen table in hushed reflection, just as we have done during every evening meal since our marriage twelve years back.

I cut into my steak. “Flesh and muscles divided like the Red Sea. The second incision, called the tour de maître, or, more commonly, *the turn of the master*, required the knife to score the curvature of the bone. The teeth of the saw detached the limb from the body, and into a bucket it would fall, turning the sawdust the color of poppies. Can you imagine that room? A muzzle of cloth soaking in the screams. Shadows dancing to the candle’s flame. Twenty-five percent of amputees died, and those who didn’t probably woke in the night to hear the cutting of bone.”

The fringe of blood around her sirloin twists her expression.

"Too rare?"

Maggie looks up from her plate, shakes her head slowly, skin wan and eyes as dark as a priest's soul.

"I love you, Maggie Kassovitz."

She always replies, "You have my heart, Gabriel."

I fetch my new acquisition from the room beyond the red door—a rosewood box, circa 1840s. Aged scalpels, chisel, lenticular, and double-ended elevator forceps used for trepanning sit within brushed velvet the color of abattoir floors. I tell Maggie how surgeons used to cut circular holes in bone, usually the skull, to help relieve pressure on the brain. For those locked in the arms of psychosis, a burr hole acted as an exit for evil spirits. And she is silent. I continue, regaling her of long forgotten practices where bloody aprons were badges of honor, and the perfume of pus lingered on skin long into the night.

No tendering of an opinion, thought, or question. I take a bite of the steak. It's salty, tender. Maggie remains mute, but from her buckled brow, I sense she wants to know how much I paid for the rosewood box.

Between bites I say, "Not as much as the poor bastards with holes in their skulls."

Chewing the steak has aggravated my back molar. The pain pulls me from slumber, and I'm pacing the bedroom floor like a nervous father in a maternity ward. Maggie no longer sleeps with me. Her side of the bed is always cold, and I think about visiting her to articulate my agony in growls and a pleated forehead. Instead, I go to the kitchen and snap a blister pack of ibuprofen. The tap water tastes like the water company siphoned it from empty graves on rainy days. I sit for a while in the living room, waiting for the pain to abate. A noise draws my attention to the communal hallway outside our front door. In a council run apartment block on the cheap side of town, it's common for the flotsam of our community to be up this late. They are vampires. Ghouls. Nocturnal wild animals. I figure a tenant with thimble guts is staggering home after hours, struggling with their keys, breath scented with kebab meat and rage. Light skulks wearily under the front door's divide like a slow-moving fog. A shadow splits it in two, and I'm leaning down to see two child's shoes, laces undone, toecaps smudged with earth. Tiny fingernails scratch our door. I raise myself up, and with a sweaty hand on the lock, lean in and ask, "Who's there?"

The scratching stops.

The shadow vanishes.

The dentist orders x-rays. Behind a surgical mask, he tells me there's no decay, abscess, or fracture in the offending tooth. Bone shows no sign of lesions, or anything else sinister that may require surgery or chemotherapy. It is a healthy virgin tooth.

"But the pain," I say, "it's unbearable."

His forehead collapses, eyes shadow with bafflement. "It may be bruxism. Has your partner ever heard you grind your teeth in the night?"

I refrain from disclosing my current sleeping arrangement.

"Are you stressed, Mr. Kassovitz?"

I reply, "Isn't everyone?"

He prescribes amoxicillin to purge the phantom infection. It's the best he can offer. That night, the pain returns, and I'm rolling on the bedroom floor crying out to Maggie, but she doesn't come. She never does.

Edna VanHalanger's house smells of cough drops and liver spots. She produces a cardboard box from under her dining table. Richard, her late husband, was a collector too, just like me. A brain tumor the size of a golf ball robbed him of his antique surgical instruments, most of which Edna sold to pay for a new conservatory. The only remaining piece is a nineteenth-century scarificator used for bloodletting.

"It has thirteen blades," she tells me. "Very rare."

I reach inside and pull out a small octagonal brass box. Edna pours tea from a cracked china teapot. I tell her how the scarificator used to make quick incisions in the patient's skin during the practice of wet cupping.

"One lump of sugar or two," she asks.

"One," I say. "A spring-loaded mechanism snaps the blades down in a circular motion, slicing the skin and issuing blood into a small cup. It was once believed bloodletting could cure heartbreak."

"How?" she asks.

"You drain the body to the point of heart failure. The heart works twice as hard to recover, and in doing so drains away the vestiges of whatever blackened it."

Richard, the recently deceased, never spoke like this to her. The scarificator, the antique magneto-electric shock machine, the Victorian bronchial kettle he polished weekly, they were all kept hidden away in a strongbox in the attic like a deep dark secret. I don't have an attic. But I do have the room beyond the red door.

Edna swears she sometimes hears voices coming from that strongbox in the attic.

"Some things remember pain," she tells me.

I know this too, but I act dumb.

"How so?" I ask.

She misses a beat. "The blood of the dead bleeds into the brass and blades. They haunt the very instruments that should have saved them."

Edna is convinced the ghosts of the dead have cursed the scarificator. I ask for the price.

"Two hundred pounds," she says, and takes a sip of tea.

I offer fifty.

She bares yellowed teeth. "Have you ever read the surgeon's warning?"

Maggie's words repeat in my mind. *The rent is due. There's no spare cash for anything that isn't essential.* The scarificator is essential.

"No," I say.

Enda retrieves a small slip of paper from a Welsh dresser and reads aloud its inscription.

"All kinds of carcasses, I have cut up. I have bottled babes unborn, and dried hearts and livers from rifled graves. And my prentices now will surely come, and carve me bone from bone, and I who have rifled the dead man's grave shall never have rest on my own."

I reason with Edna that if the surgeon's blade is a prism trapping the spirits of the dead, then surely she would want it out of her house.

"Maybe we can come to arrangement," I say.

"What kind of arrangement, Mr. Kassovitz?"

It's the hour of the wolf, and the tooth is calling out to me again. I kneel on the kitchen floor like I'm praying, the cool linoleum helping to temper the pain radiating into my cheek.

I tell myself. the painkillers will kick in soon.

I think about waking Maggie, but I listen to my tooth and all the sounds of the night. Amid the chorus of ambient noise, there is the faint sound of crying. It seems to be coming from the room beyond the red door. The closer I get, the louder the noise. The door handle chills my palm as I slowly turn it. The pain in my face is a hot poker, and I collapse on the linoleum again, growling. Under the red door, I see the wheels of my mother's chair.

At the time father ran away, Lymphedema got into my mother's legs, swelling them up so badly I'd have to cut her shoes down the middle so her feet could fit inside. Some days she couldn't walk. I found a wheelchair in an old antique shop owned by a man who suffered with psoriasis, where snowflakes of skin rested on nearly everything he had touched. The wheelchair was in the back, rusted wheels, wicker the color of tooth decay. Mother loved it because I spent the summer oiling its spokes and polishing its seat. She passed away in that chair, and I remember how peaceful she looked, like she was recalling all the times I pushed her around the village and told her she was my heart. This same wheelchair is now rocking back and forth in the room beyond the red door, like someone is sitting in the seat. An eye appears behind the gap, looking straight at me, and I reel back and scramble to the opposite wall. I rest with knees tucked into my chest, trying to comprehend the truth, the awful truth, that what I just saw was a child's eye, glazed in tears.

"Impossible," I announce to the night.

I return to my bed and hide under the covers until the wheels of my mother's chair rest, and the tears of a crying child dry up.

A different dentist stares at my previous x-rays. A bun of hair the color of choux pastry sits on top of her head. Skin smells like infidelity. She concurs with the previous evaluation, and I explain how it's been nearly two weeks without a decent night's sleep.

"The trigeminal nerve runs from the temple to the jaw," she tells me. "It can trigger sensitivity in a tooth, and pain like an electric shock. That may explain the discomfort you're experiencing, Mr. Kassovitz."

I tell her the pain is more like an invisible fist burrowing into my cheek, not an electric shock.

"I can assure you," she says, "The tooth shows no sign of fracture or decay. The only viable explanation is trigeminal nerve damage," she repeats. "Amitriptyline can help with the symptoms, but unfortunately, I cannot prescribe it. You'll need to make an appointment to see your doctor."

As she says this, the forked tip of a lizard's tongue slips from under her surgical mask, sniffing the air like the serpent in Eden's garden. My eyes articulate the shock, and she asks if I'm okay. I'm about to reach out to touch the tongue, but it retreats into the mask again.

"I'm tired," I say. "That's all."

Thursday is pizza night. I tell Maggie that they call this type of nerve damage the suicide disease.

"The pain gets so bad that you can't live with it. If the drugs don't work, surgery is an option." I wipe cheese grease from my chin on a paper napkin. "But that involves opening the skull and cutting into the membrane to access the trigeminal nerve. There's also a slight chance of permanent facial numbness."

Concern shadows Maggie's expression.

"It'll be fine," I say.

A sound draws her attention to the red door. Perhaps it's a child crying or the rusty wheels from my mother's wheelchair again, but the ballad of the kitchen is constant, a sound of a clock's hands, the gurgle from the refrigerator, the splintering in the hull of a marriage slowly sinking.

"I love you, Maggie Kassovitz."

She turns away from the red door and says, "You have my heart, Gabriel."

That night I awake to the tooth song, and its chorus of agony has me sucking air and driving my fists into the mattress. In the room's corner are figures robed in shadow, eyes glowing from the murk like cats in car headlamps, and I tell myself it's just a dream, or the consequence of sleep deprivation. But I hear them giggling as they observe me in intolerable agony.

The doctor asks questions about the pain. He is young with kind eyes, softly spoken. I decanter everything the dentist said. He prescribes ten milligrams of Amitriptyline to be taken before bedtime.

"You can double-dose if the pain gets too much," he says.

He writes out two further prescriptions—one for five hundred milligrams of Naproxem to help reduce inflammation, and Lansoprazole to counter the increase in stomach acid. As he hands them to me, black ink clouds his eyes, leaving them infinite. In the reflection, I see a terrified version of myself staring back. He opens his mouth slowly, like he's going to tell me something, but he is silent as a goldfish. Face muscles strain as his jaw dislocates with a loud snap, and the skin around the mouth rips away so I can see every tooth in his head, each one a cauldron from which a miasma of putrid smoke twirls upward. The room fills with the stench of shit and decay, and I cuff my nose. He is an anaconda feeding on a goat—a cave swallowing daylight. I stumble from the chair and walk backwards out of the room, and I hear him call out my name in a hiss.

"Kaaaaasssssaaoooovitz. Kaaaaasssssaaoooovitz."

I run from his office, almost knocking over a nurse carrying vials of blood. In the reception area, the stench of rotting teeth gives way to burning flesh, and sitting in chairs reading *Woman's Weekly* and GQ are the charred bodies of waiting patients, skin so blackened it smolders. Scabs the color of licorice fall from their limbs, and as soon as they see me enter, these burnt corpses all look up with mouths agape, atrophied tongues wagging, and red, raw skin flapping. I run out into the daylight, almost stumbling into the road where a passing bus filled with ghouls chained to their seats scratch at the window and scream, but I can't hear them over the fucking beating of my heart.

"Kaaaaasssssaaoooovitz. Kaaaaasssssaaoooovitz."

There he is, standing in the surgery's doorway, the kind doctor with slackened jaw and black eyes, one long bony finger pointing toward me as if I am all the evil in the world. Behind him shuffle blistering corpses, some holding the charred hands of children, some burnt to the bone, and as I run from this Hell, the wind crawls into my tooth and it is an ember in my mouth. I tumble and stumble and people in the street gape and gawp and shelter their infants behind walls of arms. Pomeranians, rat terriers, and Affenpinschers on their master's leash turn into jackals, hissing my name through exposed teeth varnished in drool. I have picked the lock to the gates of Hell, and I am screaming as I run with a stitch back to our apartment block.

I telephone the dentist and insist they wrench this fucking tooth from my gums before the day is done, but they proclaim the tooth is fine, and they cannot heal what is not hurt.

"Then I'll do myself," I tell them and hang up.

Beyond the red door, the clicking of wheelchair spokes chills my skin. But salvation lies within, I tell myself. Next to the four bladed vaginal speculum, the pistol grip amputation saw, the ebony handled mouth gag, and eyelid retractor, is an ivory handled tooth key, its end shaped into a claw that attaches to the tooth. With one slow turn, it will yank this bastard of a thing from the gum. All I need is whiskey and Maggie to help turn the handle.

"Maggie. Help me."

She is sitting at the kitchen table with dark eyes, skin so pale it looks transparent.

"Pull this tooth from my head before I lose my mind!"

I plead and beg, and in a whisper, she says, "You have my heart, Gabriel."

Maggie rises from the table and joins me at the red door. I feel how cold she is even though we are not touching. Hinges squeal loud as a cesspool rat as the door opens, and inside, shelves hammock under the weight of wooden boxes conceived by purl and chisel a hundred years ago. Two ropes hang from the ceiling. White blankets mimicking ghosts give form to what rests beneath. A photo nailed to the wall—Maggie sitting in a garden chair holding our son, Henry. Two milk teeth missing, fringe as gold as a wheatfield during harvest, and like the song goes, may you remain forever young.

Maggie walks into the room and waits beside the smaller blanket, sorrowful as a dog beside its master's grave.

"I was ill. I didn't know what I was doing."

She continues to stare at the blanket. Two tiny feet as white as bird bones peek from the hem.

"He wouldn't stop crying," I say. "Neither of you would stop fucking crying."

She pulls away the blanket, unveiling a bronze hook buried deep into the flesh of a boy who never made it to nine years. She then does the same with the larger blanket, and before me are the desiccated remains of my wife and son with sunken eyes and a yellowed autopsy signature scored by blades forged in the eighteenth century.

Tears stream down my cheeks as I tell Maggie that I'm sorry, and like the kind doctor, her mouth opens wide. She hisses her loathing for me, and carried on her breath is the stink of graves, of blood, and decayed flesh.

A chill comes over me, and I turn to see phantom hands of all those I have murdered reaching from the kitchen's gloom. They grab my arms, legs, and drag me screaming to the table. In chorus, they speak my name—*Kaaaaassssssaaoooovitz. Kaaaaassssssaaoooovitz.*

Henry, my sweet little boy, is down from the hook and holding the hand of his mother, and they both watch over my trial with eyes so black they remind me of inkwells.

Kaaaaassssssaaoooovitz. Kaaaaassssssaaoooovitz.

If my name is the refrain, then Enda VanHalanger chaunting the surgeon's warning is the music. *And my prentices now will surely come, and carve me bone from bone, and I who have rifled the dead man's grave shall never have rest on my own.*

"Maggie… please! Stop them!"

But she says nothing.

I turn to my boy. "Henry. Help me!"

Henry hides his face in his mother's belly.

The dead surround me, and they are many and haunting with crooked smiles and necklaces of scars. Many have holes in their skulls, and a woman in a wedding dress holds her intestines before her like a bouquet. The dealers, the pimps, the lonely and mad, the heartbroken, depressed, vengeful and sad, they were all my victims, and before I can implore and atone, they prize my mouth open with cold dead fingers wreaking of loam. Edna appears from the crowd holding the tooth key. She clamps its claw around the tooth and slowly turns the handle. The sound of metal crunching enamel is akin to ice dropped in warm water, and I am screaming like a witch burning at the stake. Pain tightens every muscle in my body as the taste of brine and pennies floods my mouth. Edna continues to turn the key, and I hear roots ripped from gum with a clack and squelch. From my mouth, she pulls the source of my misery and appraises it like a jewelry maker. My tongue hesitantly dips its head into the hole within my gum and instantly retracts as a white-hot spear of pain runs through my jaw. More agony awaits as a young man I once scalped carries in his hands the rosewood box containing the trepanning set. I apologize for my transgressions, for cutting the top off his head, but blood drenches my words.

He opens the box's lid, and presses the crown saw into my skull. The toothed edge cuts into the flesh, and I scream the house down, and wonder why the fuck no one is banging on the door or calling the police. But this is the place where the dregs and drunks, and whores and pushers dwell. Screaming is commonplace, as is the stench of death.

Wasn't that why you chose to live here? Is it any different from a wolf sleeping near a meadow of sheep? Easy grazing?

Many icy hands are upon me, ripping away my clothes, scalpels at the ready. A naked woman with two bloody stumps where her breasts used to be, draws a rusty blade over my scrotum until I sound like two cats fighting. This whore who once propositioned me is now a child digging in a bag of marbles. I don't want to look down, but I do, and she is holding the severed pearls of my fertility in her hands, smiling.

Edna rests a sternal saw upon my naked chest, scoring the skin with its toothy grin. And the percussion to my falsetto voice is the rusty wheels of the Victorian wheelchair clicking and squealing. She lifts the saw away as phantoms pull me from the table and sit me in the chair like a prisoner on death row. Maggie stands with Henry, watching.

The ghosts wheel me into the room beyond the red door, morbid faces bent with revulsion. Maggie undoes her blouse. Henry unbuttons his shirt, the one with tiny cartoon dinosaurs chasing each other. The gaping holes, where once their hearts beat for me, are now cavernous and fringed with maggots. Regret spills from my mouth in equal measure to the blood leeching from my tongue, but their expression is empty, wooden. I am a stranger, a weird apparition that makes no sense to them. I extend my hand for my boy to take, and for a moment I think Henry will reciprocate, but he ambles over to the table instead, busily searching through the various tools of my collection, each one now jellied in my blood. Through fetid breath, I articulate the knowledge gleaned from my obsession.

"Before anesthesia… amputation was an art form," I say to Maggie. "Do you remember?"

Henry returns holding something resembling a hunting knife fringed with a small chain. He hands it to Maggie, and she gently presses her palm to his face.

Good boy.

"Surgeons… they needed to cut through bone quicky. The

hammer and chisel… or jolts from poorly made saws… it was too much for many to endure."

Henry approaches, expression as blank as a river pebble.

"They needed… They needed something that could split… the flesh… and separate the bone before the patient died… because of the pain."

His tiny hands divorce one side of my blood-soaked shirt from the other. The skin beneath cleaved where Edna drew the sternum saw over my chest.

"Bernhard Heine… he changed all that when he developed… the osteotome."

Maggie joins Henry. They listen, waiting for me to finish my lecture on the osteotome, the same instrument Maggie now holds in her hand.

"It would be later known… as the very first chainsaw."

The long steel spike used to steady the device is pressed into my chest wound, and I almost choke on the scream that rips through my throat. Maggie's waxen hands grip the ball-mounted handle and turns it, setting the chain into motion. And this thing that I scoured all four corners of England for is now cutting through my muscle as easily as a caterpillar consumes a leaf. When Maggie stops turning the handle, Henry's fingers explore the expanding hole, and fingernails that once brushed the whiskers on my face now scratch at the bone protecting my heart. Give me fire and brimstone. Give me a thousand lashes from the cat-o'-nine-tails, for nothing can compare to this. Maggie turns the handle again, and the chain chews away. The crack and split of bone are the sound of logs on campfires, and the pain is as hot as the flames within. I implore Maggie to stop. To please relent and end my suffering.

"Show me… mercy, please… for old time's sake."

Her hand releases the handle. The clang of the osteotome striking the floor is a sweet melody. Before I can gather my breath, before I have time to immerse myself in the reprieve of this torture, Henry's hand quickly reaches inside the gaping hole in my chest. A crippling tightness robs me of my voice. Light diminishes. And the last words I hear are that of my son's sweet voice whispering close to my ear.

"You have our hearts, Daddy. But now we have yours."

RAGING IN THE DARK

by J. Daniel Stone

Aimee tore the sticker off a mailbox on Hester Street and placed it on the back of her phone. *Raging in the Dark*, printed in an intricate typeface. *Acid*, she thought. *Snot*. This dragged her eyes toward the sticker's detail. Mostly bone and shadow, some vague elements of violence; an insidious invite being the address was almost too small to see. But she knew the place, as one should when they've been penning stories about the dying downtown art scene for the last decade. Writing what these artists said to her, pretending for far too long that what she did was journalism.

This new lead for *Debacle*, an online blog dedicated to subterranean culture. Covering this would be the chance of a lifetime. Someone had taken careful steps to imprint these grotesque images in her head, and that said a lot. Times have changed since the pandemic. Attention spans have been reduced to seconds and people have become less creative. Artists are harder than ever to nail down. The community tends to be cliquey, so she was lucky to have landed the interview at all.

She reached the tenement at midnight. Not exactly what she expected, or even remembered. Its edifice was aged, as if it was a living thing on its deathbed. The entranceway was decrepit, and its windows were smashed, which littered the ground with wood and glass. No indication that a show was happening tonight. Graffiti was the only sign of life, an ironic display of macabre caricatures and complaining poetry. But Aimee was used to meeting in weird places, just another day in the life of a writer.

That only made her want go inside faster.

"You're the journalist."

The gallery was dark and hot, not the sophisticated squalor one expects when in the presence of artists. *Blogger*, she wanted to say, *print is dead*. Already on her second IPA, so bitter her tongue curled away with each sip. But the offer was not to be refused if she wanted this story at all.

"My name's Aimee."

The two artists and their lover sat in the shape of an isosceles triangle. Ritual in manner, but lazy in execution. Atticus at the vertex point, Dexter and Zephyr at the base angles. A rich incandescence filled the room, covering her subjects as if with a blanket, nothing to see other than hair dye and multipierced orifices.

"Aimee is a good name."

"I recognize you from social media," she said.

Dexter ran a fingernail through lightning-white hair, picked out a cigarette and proceeded to smoke it. After the initial inhale, he curled his finger for Aimee to come closer. The three pale smears watched her inquisitively, their too-white teeth greeting her with caution.

"This way."

It had begun to rain. Water sizzled against one of the windows Aimee was eyeing. An empty city is all she saw, much like this empty gallery, as one of the artists motioned her to proceed. She clambered over beer bottles, broken speakers and a pile of matte-black wood that could have once been a stage, perhaps a dais. Aimee dragged her finger through cobwebs and clotted dust, acknowledging the abandonment. She was now in the center of the gallery, or what she assumed to be the center given the panoramic view she had of the dilapidation. There were no stage lights or footlights, so she had no idea how an audience would be able to see should a show happen.

"Why's it so dark?"

"Imagination is part of the fun here. Try it."

Aimee closed her eyes, focused on a single image, suddenly able to see how easy it could have been to wow an audience from this spot, create a circle of flesh around some fierce performance artists, a three-hundred-and-sixty-degree view of a grotesque sculpture. In her mind there was plenty of neon and LED to brighten half the space, while the rest of it lived in black.

Rage in the Dark

At the last step, her heel punched through a canvas. One of the artists let out sneer, and that's when she felt something cold wrap about her Doc Martens. Looking down, she saw a weird subject revealed, gaping jaw and gore winking where its eyes had been forcibly extricated. Aimee felt a pang of embarrassment, but then quickly realized this place had fallen long ago, and thus its original creators must not have cared about whatever was left behind.

“Is there a show planned?” Aimee asked.

“Maybe.”

“Then what’s the sticker for?”

“Cheap advertising,” Atticus’ voice was low, almost muffled by the darkness.

“You’re not as spooky up close,” Aimee said.

“Social media and the person behind the account are always different.”

Aimee ignored that last part. “You’re a throuple, right?”

“Yes,” as six eyes turned in her direction.

“What does that say about the Queer community?”

“You tell me, lezzy.”

Aimee was silent.

“You think we didn’t know?”

“This isn’t about me,” Aimee said.

“Aren’t you here for a conversation?” Dexter handed her a cigarette. “Otherwise, what’s the point?”

“I don’t have any comment.”

“That’s the worst thing people in your field can hear, isn’t it?”

That wasn’t exactly false, because if nobody talked, she’d never have sold her stories to *The Village Voice, New York Press* or *CityArts,* pretending to be a journalist, reporting on gentrification and New York’s tanking creative culture, when all she ever wanted to do was write about forward-thinking art. So many years wasted writing somebody else’s story, seeking approval from editors and publishers and readers who just didn’t understand. What did they really know about power? What did they understand about the genesis of manifestation? If they felt the *change* art could bestow upon a patron, they’d have let her write that story.

“May I sit?”

"Anywhere you please."

But there was nowhere to sit. At her feet Aimee saw an X-Acto blade, a chisel, and a sketch book cradling two broken pencils. Weapons to some, just stuff to others. When she took two steps back, her boots hit into another uncomely mix of Victorian furniture, paperback books and jugs of acrylic paint that made her feel as if she was in the presence of a split personality rather than of careful artists. It was hard to imagine this place was once an epicenter of performance, as it had so easily devolved into this old dark husk.

"Goth Paris Hilton. Isn't that what they call you?" Zephyr said.

"Unfortunately."

"Do you like that moniker?"

"Let's talk about the sculptures," she said.

Aimee found a chair so she could finally get some notes down. The legs wobbled and the cushion spit dust as she sat, but after a few minutes of toying with it, she balanced herself. The artists remained on the floor. Maybe it was better down there, closer to hell. Maybe that's why the artists were so adamant to sit for the interview rather than stand. She noticed one of them eye the sweat dripping down her bare leg, not in a sexual manner, as these men were all queer, but looking *beyond* the fold, through her soul, as any inquisitive person would.

"What is that?" Aimee pointed to a baggie of opaque powder in Zephyr's hands as he packed it into a vape pen.

"DMT," he said, slowly brushing sky-blue hair away from his pointed face. "Thirty seconds of intense hallucinations."

Aimee made sure to jot that in her notepad, still too wary to use her phone to take notes, always some persistent worry that it would get deleted. Consider it the millennial mystery of growing up with technology, while at the same time being fostered by the backbone of the old school Gen-X way.

"Can I smoke some?"

"You should, yes."

Atticus stood as Zephyr said this, X-Acto blade drawn to pick out some crud beneath his fingernails. She perceived him as being much taller from what she saw on social media and somehow skinnier. But the man was beguiling in person, and he commanded a gloomy grace she had not seen in quite some time. Pale, heavily tattooed, shining hair like a crow's feather, and facial features so jagged you could sharpen knives on them. He set the blade on the table.

"For my work," Atticus said.

Another sculpture? she wanted to ask. *Give me the grand tour*. But she knew better than to bother artists about what they were working on until they were ready to talk about it, let alone demand anything. Artists can be either your best friend or your condescending enemy. There was never any way to tell until you spoke to them, and that was if they spoke at all, as most had their work speak on their behalf.

"Do you like the sticker?" Dexter was too close to her ear now, and she could smell his smoky breath.

"Very much," Aimee said, leaning away. "I've been to *Raging in the Dark* shows before, but none of you were there."

"Don't be scared of me," Dexter said. "I'm no different than you. And we've always been there, always will be."

"I'm not afraid."

"What made you think we'd even be here now?" Atticus cut in.

"Gut feeling."

"You think we like to do what we do in this shit hole?"

"It's possible."

"Well, we don't."

Dexter motioned for Zephyr and Atticus to walk with him. Aimee trailed closely behind, through a narrow hallway that felt like it would go on forever. She smelled incense, fresh dirt, and wet wood. Her ears popped as if she were winding down into a very deep basement. When they stopped, Dexter showed Aimee something he was working on. A monstrous sculpture made from resin and clay; hominid in shape but moving like a cephalopod in the way it seemed to sway between reality and dream.

"We call this *The Witness*," Dexter said.

Aimee jotted more notes, thinking how even at such a rudimentary stage, this new structure would lead Dexter and Atticus to new creative highs, but also muse-killing lows. Like a drug, the feeling one gets when creating only lasts for so long. When it's expunged, you're left stranded in a black ocean of withdrawal and emptiness.

"Is that what caused the destruction?" Aimee's face got hot with excitement.

"How did you know about that?"

"She's a journalist," Zephyr said. "Not a sycophant."

Dexter looked Aimee directly in the eyes. "If you want the real story, you'll have to sit back and listen."

Dexter placed The Witness down. Two pillar candles were the sole source of light, which only made the piece feel darker than it really was. A hellish spectacle in tangible form. The way it genuflected reminded Aimee of a gargoyle, little hands asking for touch; its nails sharp enough to draw blood. The mouth opened to rows of jagged teeth, and the face scowled so negatively she couldn't bring herself to accept it. Its paunch was twisted in metallic mummification and a sharp piece of steel impaled it upon small metal dais as if it was in the act of throbbing. Then The Witness looked at her viciously with its plucked out eyes, which caused the cheeks to appear sunken, and so she turned away.

"We survived," Atticus inhaled the DMT and then blew it in

Aimee's face. "That's what hurts the most—knowing we'll have to face it again."

Ten years ago, Aimee dragged her unwanted lesbian ass out of white trash Long Island and slid into the smoggy silver runway that is New York City. Too old to be considered a runaway, but not so unkempt that one would call her a transient. She never called her parents, and they never came looking for her. Not that they wanted anything to do with their weird lesbian child.

Anything was better than Long Island with its perfect houses, its perfect people. Aimee quickly grew sick of following rules and never being allowed to dream; the banality of it all bored her. She never fit in, and never imagined she could. So, it didn't matter that she had only fifteen dollars to her name, a dream to become a writer, and no friends to help her along the way. She was gone the second she found the courage.

The streets of New York City were not as unwelcoming as she thought. Aimee learned quickly that the key to survival was to mind her own business. The shelters had rules, they even turned the lights out at night, which meant she wasn't able to write. She adapted to sleeping in doorways and begging for change when she needed cigarettes or coffee. There were enough junkies to learn these simple tricks from, which saved her from using her body to earn money, as some of the old timers had told her to do.

A few months later she met Leila, a freelance writer who had a fascination for loose clothing and dark sunglasses. She was guided by a secret intelligence behind big, brown eyes and took Aimee on as a mentee, despite her disinterest in tabloid journalism. Leila listened to the man for a quick buck, and she was making a name for herself, but to the detriment of rigidity and conformity, whereas Aimee was determined to make her name by being rather chaotic. Leila was seven years older and had the connections to set Aimee up with editors and publishers from the small art magazine world. But for them there was always an external struggle between two different mindsets.

"You're obsessed with being *authentic*," Leila would say. "You won't make a dime that way."

"I'll do what I want."

And so, Aimee went on to sell stories to any market that would take them. Writing whatever the audience demanded. It was good practice. It was a way to make a name for herself before she knew it would time to reveal her true colors.

"You'll never amount to anything with that attitude."

Leila had a way with words, whether they were on paper or shooting from her mouth like bullets. They were words to be believed, because when you let someone into your soul, you give them access to your ego and beliefs. And when you let someone control that, you become their pawn. *I'm your life, not your stories.* Leila couldn't have been more wrong, because Aimee knew what she felt when she was writing them. It didn't matter if she sold them or not, there was something between those lines, an unexplainable satisfaction.

"One day your obsessions are going to bring the wrong people into your life."

"I'm fine with that, so long as they're interesting."

"They'll ruin you, but you're too blind to see it."

Unlike Leila, Aimee didn't treat writing as a means to an end, as a day job to just get by. It didn't matter New York City was the most soul-sucking place on the planet. It didn't care if you have no money, it still wanted its rent. It didn't care if you had a death in the family or needed time away from work to recover from a mental breakdown, didn't care if you were simply hungry. The streets were just on the other side of the wall if you couldn't pay your own way.

This place would get you one way or another.

But this place could also *elevate* you.

The art world Aimee inserted herself into was vivacious and daring, laced with the flavor of the fading underbelly of New York City. It challenged her and was unlike anything she'd ever seen. No matter the gallery, the show or performance, her eyes were pried open, lids held back with stitches. There, she was introduced to all kinds of drugs and decadent liquor, things that helped her examine everything on her end of the fork rather than getting lost in the idiocy of the world's problems.

Mind opening experiences allowing her to let go the guilt of being a failure, of falling in love too early and relying on someone who wanted to share a life without respecting her needs. Being herself was most important, the rest would follow. The circles she was part of felt more like a family than actual blood lines. *Chosen family*, they called it, and she knew this way of life would be it until she slipped into the great and endless nothingness. And her view of reality quickly changed after seeing some artists take their craft to new levels.

Aimee recalled a woman who tested the limits of human flesh by putting hooks in her skin and suspending herself in the air, until the final time she went too far and slit her own throat, skin parting and fatty red tissue vomiting from the force of her own weight. Aimee remembered the smell of metal and screaming, the hotness of blood wetting her face. It was the first time she realized people would, and could, die for their art, and the audience wanted *more*.

There was a painter whose work made it seem as if it was watching you rather than you observing it. One of his paintings, a black hole ringed in teeth, had clamped on the painter's drawing hand and severed it clean. The look on his pale face was not aghast, not shock. It was consummation. There was the dancer who reinvented body-art-movement and bent his body in ways that nature didn't intend, until one day too many bones snapped, burst through his skin, and he was unable to dance again. Tragic quests to satiate desire. Ironic failures of losing everything you lived for by simply doing what you loved. There was a name for it.

Raging in the Dark

Aimee penned stories about these darkly fabulous people, their equally dark mediums of art and haunted executions. But Leila was always there to complain about it, so one day Aimee left. Two years together, two years of clashing personalities and opposite wants, no longer holding onto the softness of that skin, the rare electricity that flared through her lips every time they kissed. No longer afraid to be alone, like when she first arrived in New York City, no longer clinging to Leila like a lifeline. It was time to start working on Aimee again, and she did just that, freed herself when she slammed the door in Leila's face that cold night, and jetted back into the familiar, endless night streets of Manhattan.

"You'll never see me again," Aimee whispered.

"You'll die for them, won't you?" Leila said.

More thunder to shake the tenement's foundation, but only enough lightning to blaze through the holes in the walls for a moment's recognition of reality. Aimee took a drag of the DMT, held it in as instructed, then let the swampy tasting smoke drift out of her nose slowly. The rain was still loud, making its own kind of music that told her soul to drift and float away.

"What do you think?" Atticus said.

"Tastes awful."

"The fun'll soon begin."

And she made sure to jot that down, a hard little scribble that would make sense once the DMT kicked in. And once it did, Aimee felt herself become engrossed in its effects. A veil seemed to be pulled over her eyes, and just as they began to adjust to the technicolor dripping, the room suddenly went black. When she came to no color was the same. Green was now a deep shade of violet, and blue a hellish red. Yellow went the way of dying flame and orange a strange necrosis. The laws of color our eyes have evolved to take in was thrown away as the DMT wound deeper and deeper into her senses.

"Is this how you do it?" Aimee asked.

"You now see," Dexter said. "Just a bit longer."

"So, is it true?" Aimee said.

"Is what true?"

"That you make your audience see things?"

"I don't know how to answer that."

"Is that why they never came back?"

"No. But the pandemic didn't help," Atticus said.

"What do you mean?"

"I don't need to explain the damn pandemic to you, do I?"

"Maybe you do."

"Wow, so snippy. Where were you when it happened?"

"On the streets," Aimee said.

"Then you should know it sent many people packing. But now

rent here is at an all-time high, it's clear New York doesn't want them back. But at least we have social media to keep connected."

"Is that how you kept your brand alive?"

"In some ways, yes. We have a big following."

"I know, I follow your accounts."

The room was now beating faster than Aimee's elevated heart rate. Dexter and Atticus had turned their backs to her, but the juxtaposition of the very white and very black hair suddenly swirled into a drifty thatch. She had to blink twice for the psychedelic effect to stop, but she didn't really want it to end. Aimee found her hand had been continuously writing, journal scrawled so roughly she'd broken through the pages with her pen, everything wet with ink. But when she looked down, she realized the wetness was not ink at all, but blood from the fingernails she'd snapped off while digging into the pages.

"What did you make me do?"

She opened her eyes to brightness, powerful heat to blast away the bad decisions of yesterday, smell of old rain filtering through her nose. Not old rain. Mold. She was still in the gallery, maybe in its dank basement, her body propped up on something hard, a stage of some sort, too blighted to support her weight but somehow it did. Something had ripped her black mini skirt, left a small red furrow between both her thighs. The blood slowly dripped into her vagina. A very small hand, from what Aimee could see, had done this.

"Behold." Dexter's voice.

There was a crowd now, hushed voices and dozens of eyes peering at her through the dark. The bodies turned as if they were one, somehow melding into a single organism, skin stitched as if a membranous quilt praising the monstrosity they encircled. Was it her? Was *she* the show? Aimee watched as an ingenue dressed in metal and latex removed herself from the living blanket, but as soon as she did, her face completely melted off her body, leaving behind only the piercings in her nose and a skeleton grin that Aimee could never forget.

"Art is too important to have anyone break the chain," Zephyr and Atticus said in unison.

"What does it have to do with me?" Aimee was unable to shift her body.

"Aren't you here to write about it?"

It was in the way the little ghoulie pranced about, the way it communicated without making a sound. *The Witness*, they named it, no rhyme or reason why. Aimee recalled its mantis legs pulling itself forward, and somehow the table it was on had changed to tall red grass, so that all she was able to see were the ghost-green depths of its eyes and the sneering rows of apex teeth. It hobbled, it crawled. She heard the crackle of its acrylic bones, the complaints of its resin paunch, the deep scratching of the metal base across the ground.

The gallery was still hot and dark, freakish tunnel vision amplifying the spectacle of journalist and subject. It's the first time she could recall taking so many notes without someone speaking. Notes in ink and blood, so many words they formed tendrils and spirals around one another. How would she make sense of this all later? Did it matter anymore? This was the majesty. This was the ultimate thrill.

And then a new sound, inside her head or imploding all around her from hidden speakers, a howling arrhythmia wanting badly to be music, but was reduced to an awful eruption of sound. The Witness reacted to this sound, pacing madly. She could see its black lips wet with black saliva, its body gyrating as if rediscovering its own instinctual movements, a dark victory for being put on display. Aimee drew closer to it, on her knees in benediction, to see the thing was writhing, realizing the music was that of its suffering.

You'll die for them

"Look at yourself."

Aimee knew the voice before she opened her eyes. Leila, pursed lips and beady brown eyes, black attire draped across her bones like wet laundry. Her hair was frayed, as if she'd she been electrocuted, and was more yellow than Aimee remembered. Back on her reprimanding bullshit and that castigating glare still so maddening. It triggered her instantly. *Nice to see you after all these years*, Aimee thought to herself. *Good to know you haven't grown as a human being*, as Leila lit a cigarette, clouding herself in the exhalation.

"Was it worth it?" Leila's question was filled with disdain.

There came the sound of a snap and sizzle. The dark dissipated. A pink glow hit Leila's face, accentuating the soft curves of her cheeks, the downturn of those kissable lips now painted violet. She always loved bright colors. The rest of the room was slathered in neon, which didn't help her to remember anything about the show, about what she'd seen, if she even saw it at all. From another part of the room there are hushed voices. *Do it again*, one of them said, followed by *I'm afraid of it.*

"You'll never write again." Leila's eyes were glazed with tears.

That's when Aimee looked at her hands, what used to be her hands. They were now many sizes too small, doll like, and the skin was not that of a human, but hard as if fashioned from resin. The nails weren't so much nails, but claws. Her tongue ran across the roof of her mouth—now more like sandpaper—until it snagged on multiple sharp pieces of metal.

"Your eyes are gone," Leila said over and over. "Your lips feel like rubber."

"I guess that's the end of the interview."

The gallery was now not so hot, a panacea of cool air coming from an unknown source. Dexter and Atticus were putting some finishing touches on *The Witness*. They didn't bid her adieu, not that she expected them to. She knew their type, not the friendliest bunch, but friendly enough to get their point across when they needed to. Thankful for the interview, she tucked her notebook into her skirt and nodded.

Zephyr escorted Aimee to the door with haste, though she didn't want to leave, not just yet. There was so much more to ask, so much more to see, to feel. But her hands were her own again, her mouth and lips the same as she'd brought into this place. The how and why didn't matter, and Zephyr was now rushing her out.

"Go now, or you can never escape it," he said two times firmly.

Aimee looked back, just a simple performance space of four walls that were falling apart and a ceiling that could come crashing down at any moment, but this place gave her something, showed her how to rage in the dark, become part of something only the chosen few could experience.

"I didn't say stop," Zephyr said again, pulling at his blue hair maniacally. "You really should go."

"She clearly wants to stay," Dexter and Atticus said together.

Then the door slammed, leaving her out in the summer rain without an umbrella.

"Don't come back," Zephyr ordered. "Write what you must, but don't come back."

No clue as to how much time she spent in there, could have been one hour or as much as a week. It no longer mattered. She found shelter from the rain in a small café, needed the time to recharge. But when Aimee went to grab her notebook, it felt larger than normal. When she looked down, her hands were shrunken, and the nails were sharp as broken glass, slicing through her journal as if it was tissue paper.

You'll die for them.

"Hello," the waitress said, approaching Aimee's table. "Are you sick?"

In the reflection of her cell phone, she saw her lips were black, eyes gone, and teeth sticking out of her mouth like tiny knives.

"Don't I know you?" the waitress said again.

NO GOD OF BREAD OR DEBTS

by Wendy N. Wagner

Dr. Keller lay on the cement floor of his laboratory, letting the cold press into his bones and make them ache. The faucet at the dogleg of the room dripped relentlessly, each tiny droplet hitting the puddle at the bottom of the basin and making a small, sharp *plip* every two and a half seconds. *Plip. Plip.* He wished he could put his head into the nearest tank to hear what it sounded like to the fish.

From below, the enormous aquariums glowed softly, the light spilling over his chest and stomach with occasional interruptions from the creatures swimming inside. Each tank held forty gallons, but space was getting tight for the oldest of the six *Ictalurus punctatus.* The Old Man spent most of his time loafing near the bottom, occasionally running his body over the rocks in an offhandedly curious way. Keller swapped the rocks every few days, just to give the channel cat something new to taste. He sometimes saw the whiskers framing the creature's nostrils trembling as it moved its side against the rocks, the motion reminiscent of a human's excitement.

Eyes still fixed on the brown and gray creature, Keller rolled up his shirt sleeve and then let his arm drop onto the floor. He sharpened his gaze at the fish as if he could bridge the gap between their minds, the hairs on his skin bristling with sensory data from the chilly substrate pressed to them. The taste buds on an *Ictalurus punctatus*'s flanks and fins would register not only the change in textures but also the chemical differences between the cement and the coarser aggregate stones, a sensitivity so far beyond a human's meager senses it sometimes moved him to tears. If there was a way to tap into the fish's abilities, it would change every field of human endeavor; the applications for mining alone would make him a fortune. Or at least, they would make the university a fortune. He'd signed away massive chunks of his rights to secure this meager basement laboratory.

A wheel rattled in the rat cages off in the other section of the lab. He sat up for a second, glad for the sound. The first experiments grafting fish hide to rat flesh had not been very successful. That the new batch of rats were up and exercising was a giant leap.

He lay back, pushing aside such thoughts. He needed to plan his next experiment, and he had doubts about its structure. He needed to dig deeper, really explore the function and purpose of *Ictalurus punctatus*'s unusual sensory organs. He needed to go to the source of his interest. Squeezing shut his eyes, he was eleven again, swimming in the thick waters of a Missouri irrigation canal. *The fish moved beneath him, the sharp spine of its dorsal fin scraping his belly. It pushed itself up from the bottom, its scales pressing against his thighs and chest as it rose. The soupy water broke over his head, and the light sparkled on the creature's scales. He was a bronco rider, a cowboy of the canal, his legs gripping its sides.* Ain't nobody gonna believe this! *he thought, and then the creature fell away beneath him.*

Keller's eyes snapped open. The memory left his heart racing, as it always did. He swallowed it down, its tiny bones tickling the back of his mind as he forced himself to focus on the here and the now. On the Old Man moving slowly in his too-small tank.

With his full attention fixed on the channel cat and the four square-inches of his own skin pressed to the floor, Keller found his senses sharpening. The concrete was powdery, tasting of the chalk sticks he'd sampled for a bet in first grade, but somehow richer than simple chalk. He thought he caught the faintest whiff of the coke-fired kiln where the lime had been heated into clinker, hot and mineral and earthen. Beside it, the gravel was nearly blindingly tangy, like licking a penny but louder. So loud he could hardly—

"Dr. Keller, what on Earth are you doing down there?"

He sat upright and stared at the staff secretary, towering over him as she never could when he was upright. He cleared his throat.

"Miss Market," he began, fumbling for words after the bliss of entering the mental realm of the ictalurus. She folded her arms across her chest. "I was studying… the movement of insects in this room."

Her lips tightened. Ten years ago, she had probably been a decent-enough looking girl but turning the corner of spinsterhood had drained the vitality from her face. Her cats-eye frames made her eyes look too far apart, and her shirtdress fit like she'd darted into the Bon Marché and snatched the first thing she'd seen on a rack. Worse, dog hair sprinkled every inch of her misshapen blue cardigan. Just looking at her made Keller want to sneeze.

Her eyes moved in a slow circle, taking in the tanks, the ceiling, the shelves on the opposite wall, and then fixed back on his face. "I don't see any insects, sir."

With some difficulty, as his bad leg had stiffened during his time on the floor, he got to his feet. She seemed to fold in on herself as he rose. She was the kind of subservient person that thrived at the edges of the academic landscape while deeply fearing their ineptness would be discovered by those larger and smarter than her. The cringing look on her face took him back to the South Pacific, the chaplain assigned to their unit. There was a man desperate for other people to make decisions for him.

Keller drew himself up square. *He* was the officer here, after all. "My fish have observed them."

She dabbed at her nose with a lace-edged hankie. "Dr. Fitzgerald sent down the latest procurement forms. I put them on your desk." She tucked the delicate square back into her sleeve. "It's awfully cold down here, sir."

"For the fish, Miss Market." He smiled, although a finger of irritation rubbed the ease from the expression. She'd had no reason for her to venture any deeper into his laboratory than the desk standing beside the door. Snoopy bitch.

She drew out the handkerchief and wiped her nose again, her eyes never leaving his face. "But what about the rats, sir?"

Keller limped past her, turning sideways to squeeze past the sink. He blinked a little at the brightness in the other half of the lab. The rows of rat cages made a maze between the fish room and the small space of his office, his surgical table waiting in readiness between the two areas. The strongly medicinal scent of carbolic acid permeated the space.

"Dr. Keller?" She paused beside the nearest cage, her palm on the grated top. "Does this rat look all right to you?" The creature stopped walking in its wheel, turning its face up to her the same way she had turned her tiny, pointed face up to him.

It was time to finish this ridiculous conversation and get back to work. "Do thank Dr. Fitzgerald for me and thank you for stopping by. But I must get back to my research." He pulled open the door and held it for her. She moved more slowly than a January turtle. "*Thank* you, Miss Market," he repeated.

She paused in the doorway, turning her unpleasant, pinched little face up at him. "Don't forget to turn in your quarterly report, Dr. Keller. The Board of Directors is holding its budget meeting next week, you know. You'll want me to type that up for them."

He forced a deep breath. Leave it to Market to hold her one scrap of power over him. She might have only been the department secretary, but she knew how to keep them all under her thumb. He could bloody well type the thing himself, but the university still insisted the secretaries handle all communications with the board. Some way to guarantee their job security, he supposed. They did little enough else.

"That's what I must get back to working on," he snapped.

"Just reminding you, that's all." She took another turtle-like step into the hallway. "And Dr. Keller—"

But he was already closing the door, which clicked shut in a very satisfying way. Her silhouette showed in the frosted glass window for a moment, one hand raised—probably still holding that disgusting handkerchief—and then she turned away, trudging slump-shouldered and lumpy down the hall.

And good riddance. Servants of the bureaucracy like her could not fathom the work he did down here. They thought fish a tedious subject and paid no more attention to them than children to their mathematics homework.

He let out the breath he hadn't realized he'd been holding. His leg quietly ached. Peace returned to the laboratory, the rumble and squeak of the wheels turning in the rat cages like a gentle tune. Keller tapped the cage beside him and smiled at the bandaged creature inside. Its whiskers twitched, a sure sign of good health. Foolish woman, carrying on about his specimens.

A glance at the clock above his desk warned Keller he'd missed lunch and would be late for his session at the pool if he didn't hurry. As much as he didn't like it, he decided it was better to use his cane than cut short his afternoon routine. The spring schedule had added a three o'clock Introduction to Swimming class, and he refused to share the locker room with undergraduates.

His teeth began digging into the meat of his cheek before he'd even made it up the stairs. When shrapnel had shredded the muscle of his right thigh, he had thanked whatever overseeing power remained in the universe for delivering him from the South Pacific. The years of recovery had shaken some of his gratitude, but he knew with certainty he would not have survived another week on that horrible island. Sometimes he still woke in the dark, his skin raw from squeezing through those underground passages, ears straining for the breath of his enemies over the chaplain's endless awful whispering of the Lord's Prayer. He found himself breathing hard and pushed back at the memory. The war was over. He was in Oregon, safe and free. The war was over.

By the time he made it across campus to the pool, his armpits stung with sweat from fighting the memories and the pain. He had to sit to change into his trunks. Back on the farm, he'd swum in his underpants, of course, as there'd been no money for special swimming clothes. Moving through those canals was the freest he'd ever felt as a boy: those rare moments when he wasn't hauling hay, or fixing fence, or looking after another lost cow. The whole of life lifted off his shoulders when he jumped into the water, just as the whole of the university and his aching leg drifted away when he dove in these days. On land, he moved awkwardly, his spine aching from the lean his cane required. In the water, he was whole. Sleek, powerful, agile. A fish.

He swam a mile and a half and then came out of the water refreshed in both body and mind. He had a new idea for the rats.

There was no point in going home, not when the work was coming along so well. Keller allowed himself a short break, making his way to the diner on the edge of campus, where he managed a glass of Ovaltine and half a roast beef sandwich. The waitress wrapped the other half in waxed paper, and he tucked it in his jacket pocket before walking back to the biology building. As usual, his leg felt so much better after his swim there was no need for his cane. He strode purposefully and comfortably in the soft spring rain, listening to the distant cheers coming off Hayward Field. Tomorrow the whole school would be a-titter with whatever new records had been set on the track, while his world-shaking work would go entirely unnoticed.

Perhaps it was better this way, he thought, finding the set of keys in his pocket and slipping into the back door of the building. The main lights had been turned off for the night, transforming long stretches of the hallways into puddles of darkness. He found himself trailing his fingers along the wood paneling as he walked, pace slowing to a creep, mind focusing more and more on the tips of his fingers. If only that flesh could be as sensate as the scales of the ictalurus, a second sight needing no light, but only contact.

The stairwell to the basement unrolled in deeper darkness. He closed his eyes, focusing his mind only on the woodgrain of the paneling. An intensity heightened deep within him, as if he could actually sense the shape of the original tree, taste the rain on skin, but then he stumbled, and it all vanished. His hand flailed on empty air before closing on the handrail. For a second, he was in the tunnels again, his men gone, the air steaming in the tropical heat. He couldn't breathe. His free hand clawed at the tie around his neck—

But of course he'd worn no tie in the jungle. He was back in the States, safe and snug in the biology building, heading toward his lab. It wasn't truly dark, not really. Once he turned the corner of the landing, he would see the dim glow of the lights in the lab, a warm, faint radiance from the window in the door.

Only as he rounded the corner, the light wasn't a faint amber as it ought to be, but a long, white rectangle spilling down the hall. Because somehow the door to his laboratory stood open.

Keller forgot he had ever been frightened. Someone was in his lab.

Someone was in his lab.

Rage boiled in his chest and he rushed forward. The floor came alive as he moved, little darting shapes that squeaked and screamed as they shot in every direction, so many he couldn't begin to dodge them. Tiny bones crunched under his feet. He burst through the door, staring in empty hope at the array of cages. Every cage save one stood open.

The woman beside them spun to face him, her eyes foolish, spinning saucers behind their lenses.

"D-doctor Keller!"

"Market!"

He lunged at her, but she dropped beneath the table and he hit only the rat cage, sending it flying. The creature inside—the last of his work—shrieked in fear.

"It's not right," she said, scuttling backward. "What you're doing. It's not right."

Keller skidded on a puddle of some unknown fluid and caught himself on the table. "Shut up."

His afternoon of brilliance: gone. Wasted. Erased by this stupid woman.

"It wasn't working," she shouted. "Fish fins on rats! The board would have shut that down, and you know it. That's why you never typed up your report."

Keller shook his head. "You don't understand."

She got to her feet, keeping the table between them. "Did you think you'd teach them to swim, too?" Her voice so mocking. How could such a pathetic, tiny little woman make fun of a man like him?

"Damn you!" He launched himself around the table, and her eyes went wide again. She spun on heel and ran for the aquariums.

He couldn't let her get to the fish. The rats were one thing, but his inspiration, his source material, that was another. His leg screamed as he ran like he'd never run, bouncing off the sink in the dogleg with a burst of hot pain. The woman had no chance. His hand shot out and at the last second before she hit the first tank, he caught her by the back of her cheap blue sweater and sent her flying. She hit the ground and rolled under the Old Man's tank.

The second adrenaline rush hit him hard and he dropped onto his belly, his fingers closing on her practical brown shoe. She kicked and flailed, but he yanked her backward. The tank wobbled as her feet and arms struck the legs of the soapstone table, water splashing everywhere, soaking their clothes.

His head broke the surface of the soupy water, the sun sparkling on the water and the great fish's scales. He hung in the air for a second as the beast turned beneath him. Its eyes fixed on him, two flat circles of brightness in the murk and the muck. The creature's enormity transfixed him, its age, its wisdom, its glacial indifference. The shape of the universe glowed out at him, two flat circles in the dark depths.

The tank rocked again, a massive wave spilling onto the floor. Gravel rumbled in the bottom, scraping and grinding loud enough Keller heard it over Market's mewling cries.

He shouted at her, but if the sounds were words, he didn't know what they formed. He reeled her in, hand over hand, her wool skirt hoisting itself over her crepey white legs, as spindly and white as the rats he'd weighed and measured that afternoon. The ones whose spines were covered in pus-filled nodules, their skin peeling off as their bodies rejected the higher order flesh he'd tried to enjoin to their inferior stuff.

Market's free leg lashed out, connecting with his temple, but he was beyond pain. He'd done this before, he knew how easy it was if he could just keep her still. He gave her another fierce yank, and now he had her, could pin down her body with the weight of his own, close his two hands around her pale little throat. She really was a rat, squeaking in fear as he held her life in his hands.

The bones in her throat collapsed so easily as he squeezed, just as his afternoon's work had collapsed beneath her treachery. The ideas he'd had in the swimming pool, so clear and perfect in the water, had eroded in the face of practical application. But it wasn't his fault.

"Do you hear that?" he gasped, tears splashing onto the lenses of her glasses. "It's not my fault."

Only a rush of wet warmth against his leg in response. He couldn't hear her little sounds anymore. In a second or two, she'd be as dead as the rat he'd stepped on in the hallway. Two inferior beings retired from their services to the University of Oregon. He wasn't sure if he was laughing because he was crying or crying because he was laughing.

It was the university's fault, of course. How could something as magnificent as an *Ictalurus punctatus* be studied under these conditions? Using these cheap and pathetic tools? God did not show himself to the unworthy. The chaplain had prayed long and loud in those tunnels and God hadn't once shown his face. Keller had covered the fool's mouth and begged him to shut up, but he wouldn't stop, he wouldn't stop, and the Japs had stood in for God with their Type 100s flashing bright.

Miss Market's mouth fell open, round and hollow and dark. This close, he noticed a long brown hair sticking out of the mole on her upper lip.

He dropped her with disgust. The room stank of piss and aquarium water, with a faint tang of horseradish from the crushed sandwich in his pocket. His hands trembled as the adrenaline ebbed out of his body.

The rats were gone. His work, ruined. He could hide the secretary's body, maybe even dump it in the river, but he was no criminal mastermind and neither was she. The university had cleaners. One of them might have seen her coming down her, might at any moment come downstairs themselves and see the mess on the floor in the hallway, the light spilling out of the lab. Even if Keller moved fast, he doubted he could tidy away all of this trouble.

He was too tired to care. Tired, but also some other, more electric feeling. The shaking spread from his hands through the rest of his body as the brighter feeling spread. He didn't know what to call it. *Inspired*, perhaps. The realization his work had hit a standstill because of the university's rules, the university's budget, had churned up something from the fecund material at the bottom of his own mind. He thought perhaps the idea has always been there, simply restrained by the strictures of budget reports and laboratory assistants and playing by the rules. When had playing by the rules ever done him any good? If he'd never broken the rules, he never would have learned how to swim, would have worked himself to death bucking hay bales and shoveling cow shit.

Even as he thought all this, his hands were moving. Pushing him out from under the fish tank, dragging Miss Market by the heels and shoving her into metal cabinet where he kept his aquarium supplies. Buying a little time for the next step.

He was already at the sink, scrubbing up with pink antiseptic soap. He had proven his worth over and over. Had been chosen for just this purpose. He hesitated for a moment beside the aquariums, but the sacrifice had to be made if he was going to take the last and biggest leap in his research. Then he slid the net down the side of the glass, scooping the fish tenderly out of the water.

"Thank you, Old Man," he whispered.

The fish's barbels moved in acquiescence or perhaps even benediction.

There was no question of taking the cane. Every inch of him ached with exhaustion after the fight with Miss Market and the long careful hours of surgery, but he had to take this walk on his own. The rain had stopped, and the campus lay in quiet darkness as he carefully picked his way beneath the trees. Every footstep made his face burn and ache.

He really should wait at least three days before testing the surgery, but he knew he didn't have that kind of time. At least the nerves were pressed together, even if they weren't healed seamlessly yet. He could already feel his mind straining to understand the new sensations in his face. He had always known it was the weakness of the human mind that kept science from truly grasping the world of the catfish, but now he actually felt his brain straining and growing and changing. His heart pounded with excitement. The improvement of the human animal was in his grasp.

The campus master key he'd earned as the department chair last year trembled in his hand. The university had asked for it back, but he'd signed papers promising he'd misplaced the thing while out of town. The operations department was all too happy not to change the locks, and he'd never abused his privilege. Some part of him must have known he'd need to do this one day. The pool wasn't the perfect place to test his work, but he knew he'd never make it down to the river after all he'd been through.

The clean, heavy smell of chlorine normally made him smile, but his lips were too swollen to move. The barbel whiskers hung down over chin, tickling slightly. He could almost taste the moisture in the air.

Very distantly, an alarm bell rang. He thought it came from the direction of the biology building, which meant he didn't have much time. He skipped the locker room and stripped down to his underwear beside the pool. There were no lights, but he didn't mind. A channel cat didn't need light to find their way in the world. Their other senses more than made up for their eyes. His fingers tingled and whispered as he lowered himself off the tiled rim and into the water.

The fish moved beneath him, the sharp spine of its dorsal fin scraping his belly. It pushed itself up from the bottom, its scales pressing against his thighs and chest as it rose. The soupy water broke over his head, and the light sparkled on the creature's scales. He was a bronco rider, a cowboy of the canal, his legs gripping its sides. Then he was falling free, the fish turning beneath him, staring up at him with the bright, flat eyes.

Every inch of his body crackled with life, with sensations and information he'd never imagined. The rich savor of his own blood filled his mouth as stitches broke and skin ripped free. He was a boy again, his father slapping him for reading in the barn. He was a lieutenant again, feeling his men slip away in the tunnels and not knowing if he crawled through their guts or some nameless Jap's. He was on the floor of his laboratory, watching the Old Man.

Focus, he told himself. *Remember the canal. Remember why you are here.*

The fish stared up at him, its eyes vast and uncaring as it measured his worth as an offering.

He pushed himself to the bottom of the pool, all the way down to the poured concrete floor. His belly scraped the surface, and he tasted the lime and minerals of it. Laughed a little to himself at the intensity of the sensation, so much more powerful than his mere imaginings back in his lab. His new whiskers floated around his face and warned him he'd swum into a corner. It was just the kind of place the Old Man liked to maneuver himself into.

His lungs began to burn, but he waited. His skin itched, but that was normal for tender scales exposed to this much chlorine. He was so close to his breakthrough. So close.

That day in the canal, he'd looked down at the great fish and seen the width of its mouth, the enormity of its body. A sense of great age and tremendous, alien wisdom rippled off its scaled flesh. He felt suddenly, unimaginably overwhelmed by how tiny he was beside this wondrous being.

The smallness of his life hit him then, the day-after-boring day of it. He, John Keller, was nothing. All his farm-boy dreams of seeing the world and being something special shrank to the point of a pin as he moved above the god-like vastness of the catfish. The best he could hope for was for it to swallow him whole.

He had *begged* it to do so, to subsume him into its great self so he could be part of that vast and ancient mystery. But instead its whiskers had risen to explore the length and breadth of his body, and dissatisfied, had turned away, vanished, never to be seen again.

Back in his bed that night, he'd cried until his eyes swelled closed. Every fiber inside him had ached from that rejection. And from then on, he'd prayed to his own kind of God when his parents demanded the family say Grace. Had looked for that scaled and merciless God when he'd been trapped in those tunnels, seething at the inane words of the weeping chaplain. As if any kind of God could be concerned with bread and debts when the world was made of darkness and mystery.

Now Keller prayed in the only way he knew. He opened his bloody mouth and forced the water in deep, deeper, all the way into the depths of him. Fear and hope burned flares in the backs of his eyes, two bright pale circles piercing the darkness at the bottom of the pool.

The fish opened its maw.

Somewhere at the surface, someone shouted. They had found his clothes, but it no longer mattered. The water was taking him. The light of God was taking him. His body bucked in pain and fear as the surface of his lungs boiled out of his throat in the pink foam of death. Finally, after all these years, Keller's God was swallowing him whole.

In Mourning, She Wakes Again

by Eric LaRocca

"A mother's soul is tested when she puts a child in the ground."

That's what my doctor had told me when my son passed.

However, little did he know that I could never bear the indecent thought of poor Gregory's body languishing in an expensive casket for all of eternity. The whole burial process unnerved me terribly and made little sense. To me, it seemed so much wiser to cremate my beloved son's body—a fiery spectacle that might balance some of the brilliant marvel that he possessed while he was alive and gracing us with his presence.

To me, darling Gregory would always remain at the tender age of eighteen. He'd forever be caught somewhere between the gracelessness of an awkward teenager and the confident certainty of a potent young man.

Of course, to others, Gregory might have been exceptionally ordinary. Young poets are usually so meek and unassuming—far too humble for their own good. To those who are unsophisticated and unable to discern greatness from the exceedingly dull, Gregory might have been considered boorish or extraordinarily average. But not to me. Gregory and I sipped from the same fountain of vitality and liveliness. Some people might have condemned us being so close, so unreservedly attached to one another. But we didn't entertain the blatant disapproval of others. To us, their criticisms were amusing. We could dine eternally on their disapprovals, judgements, wordless convictions. That is, until Gregory perished unexpectedly last autumn, and I was left to endure the gossip—the all-consuming talk.

I hardly wanted to chat with anyone, least of all what I expected to be a phone solicitor calling at dinner time.

"I'm sorry," I said, answering the phone. "We're not interested."

A young man's voice greeted me on the other end of the line. His voice was soft, as if he were speaking through a sheet of wax paper. He had a gentle lilt to his tone, almost identical to the way Gregory once spoke.

"Is this the Pierce residence?" he asked.

I collected myself, a little surprised by the gentleness of the young man's voice—perhaps a little surprised by his ability to remain so composed despite my mercilessness.

"Yes," I said. "If you're selling something, I'm afraid I'm only going to disappoint you."

"I'm not selling anything, ma'am," the young man said. "I'm looking for Gregory Pierce. Is he there?"

Little moments of despair like these creeped up from time to time—horrible moments when I was reminded of the enormity of my loss. I imagined that losing a beloved child was like breaking a bone that might one day heal again, might one day repair itself until it's functional once more. But, to me, losing Gregory was like amputating a limb that would never grow back.

"Are you a friend of my son's?"

"I am," he said. "My name's Conrad. I went to high school with Gregory."

"Pembrose Academy in Cheshire?" I asked, delighted to recite the school's name once more and eager to start singing the academy's anthem.

"I was on the rowing team with your son," Conrad said. "We went to the state finals together."

I sensed myself smiling a little at the memory. "Yes. I recall. He detested that I made him take up a sport. But he loved all the friends he made on the rowing team."

There was a brief silence on the other end of the line, as if Conrad was somewhat uncertain how to accept my sentimentality.

"When did you graduate?" I asked.

"Same year as Greg," Conrad said. "We went to senior prom together because our dates were friends."

I recalled the evening when Gregory escorted the young Davenport girl to prom. I thought of how handsome he looked in his black tuxedo and how much I loathed his blonde-haired companion—detested her actually. Of course, I knew it wouldn't be acceptable for me to accompany Gregory to the event. I certainly never wanted to embarrass him or make his life more difficult than it had to be because so many others could already see just how sensitive and delicate he was. The world has never been kind to delicate things—least of all young men who are decidedly feminine in their appearance and demeanor. In fact, if you're delicate or sensitive in any way, it's almost too glaringly obvious the world wants to destroy you. That's what it did to my poor Gregory, after all.

"You must be young?" I asked, uncertain how he might react.

"I'm nineteen," Conrad. "I've been studying English literature at Bennington College in Vermont."

For a moment, I felt safe, as if I were suddenly very much aware that I was talking to someone just as tender and as thoughtful as Gregory.

"That's a lovely school," I said.

"Is Greg around?" Conrad asked. "I haven't talked to him in over a year or so."

What to say? Surely, I couldn't tell this perfectly polite young man that Gregory was deceased and had been since last autumn. For some inexplicable reason, the truth seemed far too ludicrous to divulge. It wouldn't make sense. More to the point, telling this perfect stranger that my son had perished made me feel as if I were responsible for his death, as if I were killing him every time I articulated the horrible truth that he was dead.

It doesn't have to be true, I thought. *Yes, why tell him and upset this polite young man?*

Certainly, I could have reconsidered. I could have told Conrad the truth, and we could have bonded the way loved ones usually do when a follower of their clan falls away to oblivion. But I felt guilty for sharing something so abhorrent, something so grisly. More importantly, I didn't want to.

"He's out at the moment," I said. "Picking up some eggs and bread at the store. Would you like me to take a message?"

Conrad stuttered a little, perhaps somewhat unsure and nervous. "I—uhm—I'm organizing a reunion with some of the guys from the rowing team. I was hoping Gregory could join. Or, at the very least, help me plan some of it."

"You're hosting a reunion?" I asked, realizing only too late that I sounded far too excited at the prospect. "Where?"

"Probably one of the coffee shops we used to visit near Pembrose," Conrad said. "Greg always had great ideas."

"Yes, he did," I said. Then, realizing, I corrected myself. "*Does*, I mean. He always *does*."

"Will you tell him I called and I'd love to see him while I'm in town?"

I thought for a moment and almost instantly an idea crept onto the carpet of my mind.

"Why don't you come over to the house tomorrow?" I asked. "We can chat and discuss what's to be done about this reunion."

Conrad seemed a little surprised and overwhelmed by my offhand suggestion.

"Yes," he said, clearing the phlegm in his throat. "That sounds—nice."

"Gregory might be in and out all day," I said. "You know how he is. Unable to sit still. But I'll let him know you're coming. Okay?"

"Very good," Conrad said.

"You have our address?"

"Yes. I think so. Any time?"

"Let's say two o'clock," I said. "I'll see you then, dear."

I hung up the phone and, for a moment, I settled into the cushioning of the armchair. It felt as though my body were somehow liquid, passing through space and time with the utmost certainty I would once again be complete and whole.

After I had composed myself, I made my way to the mantle on the opposite side of the dining room. There, I located the small urn where I'd deposited the cremated remains of my beloved Gregory. As I've done many times before, I pushed my index finger into my mouth and gently wetted the tip until it was dripping with spit. I unscrewed the lid of the urn and lowered my damp finger until deep inside the mound of ash—all that remained of my darling Gregory.

I dipped my ash-covered finger beneath the waistband of my underwear and gently teased the hairless area between where my thighs met. I rubbed him there—aching to feel something, even if that feeling was utter disgust in myself for what I was doing, the longing I continued to feel for my beloved Gregory.

Conrad showed up on my doorstep at precisely two o'clock in the afternoon.

Before I opened the door, I glanced out the window beside the entryway and took in the sight. He was a little heavier than I had imagined and seemed to be somewhat self-conscious about it from the way he slouched, as if trying to make himself appear smaller than he was. His face was pockmarked and freckled with new acne, his hair parted and slicked to one side. He adjusted the spectacles sliding down the tip of his nose. Despite some of his obvious shortcomings, he captured the quintessential boyish charm Gregory had once possessed—that indescribable youthful vitality all young males seem to carry.

I flung open the door and Conrad greeted me with a sheepish look.

"Mrs. Pierce—?"

"Please. Come in, dear," I said, ushering him across the threshold and into the foyer. "May I take your coat?"

He immediately shrugged off his jacket and passed it to my open arms. While he momentarily turned away, I inhaled the scent clinging to his coat—fresh pine needles, patchouli, and cologne.

Of course, it didn't bear a resemblance to the scent I had been accustomed to whenever near Gregory. My son carried with him the most bewitching scent—a scent that always perplexed me and yet enchanted me so.

I had once read somewhere animals in the wild release certain pheromones so that their parents know not to mate with them. In fact, some of the other mothers I had chatted with at the school bake sales constantly lamented at the unique and abhorrent smells of their sons. I never understood to what they were referring. To me, Gregory would always be the epitome of perfection.

"Come into the parlor, dear," I said, hanging the young man's coat on the nearby rack and then leading him through the doorway. "I've already made some tea for us."

"That's very kind of you," Conrad said, hands fumbling nervously as if uncertain if he should shove them in his pockets or let them dangle at his sides. "Will Greg be joining us—?"

"Greg had to run a quick errand," I told him, turning away so he couldn't notice the lie scrawled across my face. "He'll be back by the time we're finished with our tea."

I gestured for Conrad to take a seat on the sofa arranged near the fireplace. I knelt beside him and began preparing a cup of tea for him.

"I imagine you and my son were very close at Pembrose," I said.

I noticed him occasionally glancing around the parlor, eyeing the pictures from expensive European vacations pinned to the walls.

"Yes," he said. "Greg often kept to himself."

I laughed, amused a little. "You know my Gregory well. You speak our language."

"But he seemed to enjoy my company," Conrad said. "We fell out of touch when we went to college. Where does he go again?"

I cleared the catch in my throat, passing the cup of tea to Conrad. "He's taking some time off this year. Too much stress. His senior year at Pembrose nearly broke him completely."

"My father would've disowned me if I had taken a year off," Conrad said.

"Thankfully, Gregory's father passed away when he was very young," I said. I'm astonished at my honesty around this perfect stranger. Still, it felt as though I had known him for quite some time, as if I were only revealing necessary things he ought to know about us. "I always encouraged Gregory to follow his heart and do what was in his best interest. A poet's path is never an easy one."

"Yes," Conrad said, suddenly looking somewhat wistful. "He was always writing those little poems in his notebooks."

"I have a collection of them," I said. "The pages are now yellowing with antiquity. But the contents are flawless. Especially my son's penmanship. I go up to the attic and read them from time to time."

Conrad winced, smiling a little. "You must be his greatest fan."

"You must be delighted to reconnect with him after such a long absence," I said. "When and where is this delightful reunion taking place?"

Conrad swallowed a gulp of tea and set the cup down on the saucer. "Tomorrow afternoon. At the park. It's such lovely weather for April, after all."

"Most excellent," I said. "And there will be others that knew Gregory in attendance?"

Conrad nodded. "Most of the guys we knew from the rowing team. They're excited to see Greg again."

I couldn't quite continue to disguise my discomfort whenever Conrad shortened Gregory's name to "Greg." It felt so demeaning, so unceremonious and insulting. I wondered if I might correct him, if I might beg him to use Gregory's full name. But I stopped myself and carried on with the conversation.

"Would it be terribly upsetting if I joined as well?" I asked.

He hesitated slightly, as if surprised I would even ask. "You join…?"

I felt foolish almost immediately. I waved him away. "It's silly. You don't want an old woman there."

Conrad looked uncertain. "If you'd like to come, you're more than welcome. It may not be that interesting to you."

"I expect you'll want to have your boy talk," I said. "I'll leave you in peace, I promise. I just would like to meet some of my son's friends. That's all."

A gentle stillness suddenly fell over us, almost as if all the oxygen had been sucked out of the room through a small valve.

Conrad stirred in his seat, glancing at his wristwatch.

"Did Greg say when he'd be coming back?" he asked.

"I expect not for a while," I said. "Why don't you come back tomorrow afternoon and we'll all drive over together to the park? You and Gregory can chit chat, and I'll keep quiet in the backseat."

Conrad didn't look impressed with the plan, but he disguised his disdain well enough for a nineteen-year-old.

"That sounds nice," he said, rising from his chair and heading toward the foyer.

Before Conrad left, there was one thing I had to know—from one of his close high school friends. Something that had been gnawing at me since we had cremated Gregory last autumn.

"Tell me, Conrad, did Gregory ever mention me to you or any of your friends on the rowing team?"

Conrad's face scrunched, obviously confused. "Mention you, Mrs. Pierce?"

"In passing," I said. "I talked—talk—about him all the time. I was only wondering if he did the same."

Conrad shook his head and offered a look that nearly ripped me from groin to gullet.

"I don't remember," he said. "I—don't think he ever mentioned you."

I tried to conceal some of my embarrassment, but part of me wondered if Conrad truly saw through some of my miserable pretense. There was every possibility he did. I certainly had every right to be as upset as I was. I had finally recognized the horrible truth—I loved my precious Gregory more than he could ever possibly love me.

The following day, Conrad arrived at noon and looked perplexed again when I answered the door. Only this time, I was dressed in a periwinkle blue negligee that my deceased husband had bought for me on one of our many vacations to Greece.

"Am I—early?" Conrad asked, checking his wristwatch.

"Nonsense," I said. "You're right on time. Please come in, dear."

I guided him into the foyer once more and took his jacket from him, hanging it beside the bannister on the coat rack.

I noticed how Conrad glanced around the house, searching for someone—anyone other than me.

"Is Greg upstairs getting ready—?"

"He'll be with us in a bit," I told him. "Why don't we have some tea in the dining room?"

Conrad laughed at the suggestion. "We'll be late."

"Nonsense," I said, wrapping my arm around his and drawing him further into the dining room. "Your friends can't do anything until we arrive."

I motioned for Conrad to take a seat across the large dining room table from me. He sat and stirred there with visible reluctance. I couldn't help but notice how his patience with me was growing thinner and thinner. He resembled how Gregory used to bristle at me, vexed and clearly annoyed whenever my coddling became too intense. I often reminded him, however, to accept my mothering with grace because the world would be too delighted to destroy such a precious and gentle thing such as him.

"I've been thinking about something you said yesterday, dear," I said, pouring a cup of tea and passing it to him. "Something about my precious Gregory."

"He's on his way, right?" Conrad asked, glancing up the stairs as if waiting to spy Gregory at any moment.

"I found it odd when you said he never mentioned me," I said. "After all, Gregory and I have always been thick as thieves. Then, it made me wonder if you were playing a trick on my beloved Gregory and me."

"A trick?" Conrad asked, sipping from the cup of tea. "I—don't know what you mean."

"It's no surprise that I knew dear Gregory had his share of enemies," I said. "People who resented him for his talents, his grace. I found it rather—peculiar—that Gregory had never mentioned you before. Especially since he always told me everything."

Conrad stammered, as if he had been caught. "We weren't that close, I suppose."

It was then I noticed beads of sweat popping along Conrad's forehead. He wiped them away almost immediately, stretching out the collar of his white shirt with his index finger and his thumb.

"You weren't close at all," I said. "I always knew who his friends were. He never spoke of you. What's more, it's telling how little you knew of him to say that he never mentioned me. We were each other's entire worlds."

Conrad's eyes bulged. He stammered as he strained to lift himself out of the chair.

"I—thought—I—didn't..."

Before he was able to finish the sentence, he collapsed to the floor. I watched in silence as his palsied hands beat tirelessly against the carpet as if straining to lift himself to no avail.

I noticed the poor boy's eyes dart to the "In Memoriam" card I had positioned on the dining room mantle, a small picture of my darling Gregory situated beside it. I observed Conrad's mouth open, drool collecting there, as he struggled to comprehend.

"He's—dead—?"

"Yes," I said, patting his back the way a mother does when she's patronizing a small child. "Do you know how he died?"

Conrad answered with an inhuman, agonizing moan.

"A car accident. The paramedics told me he never felt any pain. He was decapitated instantly."

The words lingered in the air for a moment, as if they were somehow telling poor Conrad what was in store for him—everything I had planned, the love I had intended to redeem.

It didn't take me too long to locate the group of young men waiting for Gregory and Conrad in the park. I found them sprawled on a checkered blanket on a grassy knoll near the base of an old sycamore tree.

At first, they didn't seem to notice me as I approached. To them, I probably resembled an old beggar woman dragging a bundle of her belongings behind her. But very soon I knew they would recognize the blood trailing across the grass after me like a livid current following a small boat when it passes across still water.

They turned to face me as I intruded upon their little gathering.

They probably didn't know what to make of me—the dried blood rusting on my skin, the way I stared at each of them with such purpose, such defiance. It was then they began to recognize what I was dragging behind me—the headless shape I had dropped on the edge of their blanket the way a house cat delivers fresh kill to their owner.

Everything around me seemed to blur, as if I were opening my eyes underwater. I sat on the edge of their blanket, the faintest sounds of screams echoing in the distance, and I began to read from the very last notebook Gregory had used before he died.

If my voice quivered, it was only for a moment and only because I wasn't used to speaking in front of large groups of people. It didn't matter now. I would be damned before I allowed Gregory's words to languish in a journal for all eternity. He would be heard, and he would be heard now.

I peeled blood-speckled pages apart with trembling fingers and continued reading each poem to the shocked onlookers. I did this faithfully until I sensed each divine word I was reciting caught on a passing breeze and carried far away to a place where our love as mother and son was the only consecrated language.

THE FALL OF FELIX ELLERBY

by Beverley Lee

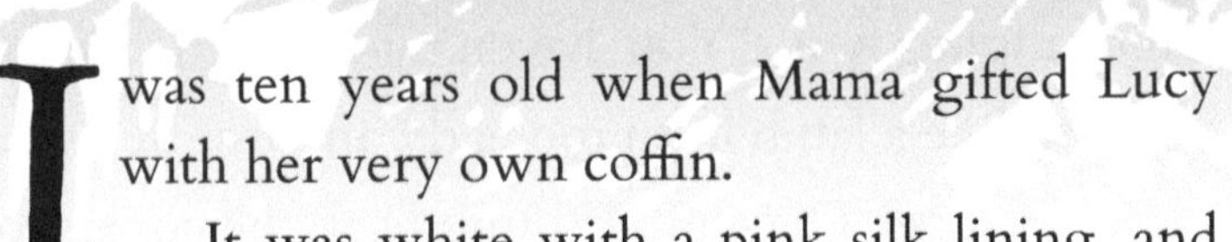

I was ten years old when Mama gifted Lucy with her very own coffin.

It was white with a pink silk lining, and it came with a doll I hated the moment I set eyes upon it. But I'm getting ahead of myself. Stories have a beginning and an end, at least that's what Miss Frobisher told us. I'm not really sure what part this is. Stories are like life, they begin and you can't stop them. They gather speed and hurtle towards a cliff, becoming stronger and more wilful, and they don't care who they rip apart on the rocks below.

Mama says I'm very morose but I just see things as they are.

I've changed. I look people in the eye now, and wonder.

I paid a price for what I did. I continue to pay the price.

But do not judge me for what you don't understand.

"Felix, wake up!" Her urgent words stole through the candyfloss land I'd been wandering in, half-awake but hoping I could steal a few more moments. Small fingers played with the tip of my nose, and I opened one eye.

The thin light of a winter dawn peeked through the nursery curtains, and I tried to pull the coverlet over my chin.

"Felix." Her tone had gone from excited to stern, mimicking Mama when we became too exuberant. "You can't go back to sleep. It's my birthday." She curled her bare toes under the hem of her white nightgown. "You haven't forgotten, have you?" Now she sounded like a lamb born too early and lost in a storm.

"Of course, I haven't." I flung back the covers so she could climb in beside me even though I'd been told that it wasn't proper. It had been fine last year but as soon as my tenth birthday came, it wasn't anymore.

I didn't care. She was my little sister and I adored her.

She snuggled close, winding her legs and arms around me like the baby monkeys we had seen in the zoo last summer. Her hair tickled my cheek. Somehow it had escaped the rags Mama had wound in it the previous evening. Lucy's hair was wild, much like her spirit.

"Do you think people miss this when they're dead?" Her voice held a sombre curiosity.

Before I had a chance to answer there was footfall on the steps leading to the nursery, at which point Lucy slipped back into her own bed, feigning a yawn as Eleanor came in carrying a coal scuttle. She set it by the hearth and cursed under her breath.

"I be late, Master Felix, but don't you go a-telling on me. That layabout, Greaves, didn't fetch the coal, and I had to go get it myself. Bloomin' liberties."

She knelt and swept the ash from the grate.

"Bloomin' liberties!" Lucy yelled with delight and I laughed so hard I nearly wet myself, whether at Lucy's parroting or Eleanor's horrified expression, I wasn't sure.

Lucy was a ball of energy as Hester supervised our dressing. Hester was small and thin with black hair shot through with white. She looked as if she would snap in a strong wind, but she was as tough as nails, and had been Mama's nanny too.

"Part of the woodwork, I am," she would mutter when anyone asked her what she did before coming to Ellerby Hall. "The only before I had was when I was nursing on my mother's tit."

Old age had gifted her with a wonderful sense of impropriety which she only showed occasionally, even though both Lucy and I goaded her mercilessly.

It was Sunday and that meant donning my best suit, complete with waistcoat and the starched collar I hated because it made my neck itch. Lucy didn't fare much better, bedecked with ribbons and a bonnet that she said meant she could only see in front of her like a carriage horse. She caught my eye as we walked the pathway to the church and neighed under her breath.

Mama gave me the most disapproving look. "Do not encourage your sister. God does not allow for frivolities, Felix."

A stiff breeze stung my cheeks, as though God was agreeing with Mama's words, and as we passed over the threshold of the church and into its cold, unwelcoming belly, Lucy wound her fingers through mine.

The sermon dragged on and on. Lucy fidgeted on the wooden pew, kicking the toes of her satin shoes against the hassocks. I had the misfortune of being seated next to Mama so had to behave as though the message Reverend Green dispensed was a gift to my innocent ears.

As we exited the church, both of us awash with relief, Mama paused to thank Reverend Green for his enlightenment.

Lucy took off into the churchyard at a speed not appropriate for a Sunday. I followed, catching glimpses of the pale blue silk she wore weaving through the tall gravestones. I found her kneeling at a new grave, her fingers tracing patterns in the recently turned soil.

"What do you think it's like, Felix? To be dead?"

Before I had a chance to answer, shouts came from just beyond the lychgate.

"There's sickness here, I tell you. I can smell it!"

The words came from a boy, a few years older than myself. He was sprawled in the dirt and wore a filthy shirt and trousers made of sack cloth. The soles of his boots were full of holes.

"Away with you, Maverick Turner. Get back to the hovel you crawled from. These are God-fearing good people and do not want to see the likes of you." Mr. Foster, one of the church elders, stood by the gate, his hands curled over the top of a walking stick.

The contempt in his voice was more biting than the winter wind.

"I tell no lies…" Maverick began to say, then scrambled to his feet, his eyes on the raised walking stick. "I saw it in a dream."

"Saw it in a dream," Mr. Foster scoffed. "You're here for coin, boy, but you'll find none."

Maverick wiped his nose on his ragged sleeve. His gaze fell upon me, standing in a wayward patch of sunlight, primped and polished with a full stomach.

He held my gaze until the walking stick cracked down against his shoulder. Then he retreated a few steps and spat on the ground.

It was something I'd seen the stable hands do but it gave me a strange kind of thrill to see a boy close to me in years show such contempt for authority.

Lucy was wild in a playful, charming way. He was wild because that was the lot life had dealt him.

"Damn him and his kind to hell," Mr. Foster muttered as he came back up the pathway from the lychgate. A few other men nodded at his words. He wiped the tip of his stick with a handkerchief as though Maverick had been some kind of disease. "Mark my words that scum should be hung now before he does something there's no coming back from."

I lingered on the edge of the conversation, one eye on Lucy as she lowered an ear to the ground, her ribbons trailing in the dirt.

"Aye, I agree. His father's in gaol now, stole a few chickens out on Laidlaw's land. I don't know where his mother is, so it's just him and a few other whelps running amuck. The whole lot of them would starve if it wasn't for people throwing them the swill that should go to the pigs."

The men laughed as though this was a hearty joke.

My stomach turned over at the thought of it.

"I hear some believe he's got some kind of sixth sense. Heard talk of him helping a family over the moor when their babe was sick with fever. But it's all poppycock. Folks will resort to anything when family hovers at death's door."

This last exchange sobered Mr. Foster up considerably, and I watched as he went back into the church to gather the hymn books.

Mama swept in, and after scolding Lucy for running off and getting dirt upon her new frock, we climbed in the carriage and headed home.

The late afternoon light was fading, and gloom gathered in the corners of the parlour, but the fire was set in the grate, and it crackled merrily. We were seated before it, still dressed for Sunday although Lucy had been allowed to remove her hat.

Mama placed a box, tied with a pink ribbon, on Lucy's lap. It was all Lucy could do not to tear the ribbon off, but she waited until Mama returned to her seat. Lucy's little fingers shook with excitement as she untied the ribbon. Mama watched on from the wingback chair, a china cup and saucer balanced on her knee.

The box had a hinged lid. From where I sat, cross-legged, I couldn't see inside, so could only watch Lucy's face as the gift appeared. Her lips parted in awe, and the flush on her cheeks deepened.

"Mama, it's beautiful!" She raised her face and the flames danced in her eyes. "Look, Felix, look!" Lucy pulled the gift from its wrappings and held it for me to see.

The coffin was perfect down to the very last detail. But it made my scalp tighten against my skull, and despite the warmth from the fire, I shivered.

"Felix, what do you say to your sister?" Mama's shoe nudged me between my shoulder blades.

I didn't get a chance to answer as Lucy had opened the coffin and the squeal of joy from her lips echoed around the room.

It was a funerary doll, dressed in teal silk with a lace pinafore. It had blue eyes that opened and closed and summer-gold hair that bore a resemblance to Lucy's own. Maybe that's why I hated it at first sight.

I knew why Mama had done it. She indulged Lucy's fascination with death because it would evolve into the necessary art of mourning, something Mama excelled in.

A boy, however, does not need to know how to grieve. My

emotions should be locked away. But the more a thing is hammered into you, the deeper the bruises go. Sometimes things simply curl up and hide.

Lucy placed the doll inside its coffin and closed its eyes. She arranged the tiny porcelain hands across its chest, then clasped her own above her heart, her expression deepening into sorrow that had no place on a child of six.

Mama smiled and sipped her tea.

I stared into the flames and felt the burn at the back of my eyes.

A few days later I came up to the nursery to get a book. My feet halted on the threshold as though they had been glued there. Lucy had lined up all her dolls with the coffin at the centre. She knelt by them, her face a mask of sombre compassion.

"Earth to earth, ashes to ashes, dust to dust," she recited. In that moment I swear I could taste those ashes on my tongue.

There was a strange odour in the room, something slightly rancid, but the window was open so I took it to be from outside.

"Do you want to go into the garden when I've finished my studies?" I forced my steps forward and grabbed the book from the shelf.

Lucy raised her head. "I can't, Felix. I have to bury Catherine."

"You've just done that," I said, a hitch of frustration to my tone. The cover of the book felt like old skin against my fingers.

"I need to do it again. It isn't perfect."

Her face lowered, blonde curls spilling over her shoulders.

I wanted to say that dead was dead, it didn't need to be perfect. Rage towards Mama burned in my gut. I hated the doll and the coffin, hated what her encouragement had done.

Lucy was asleep by the time I slipped into bed, which was unusual. She liked to stay awake so I could tuck her in and check under the bed for monsters.

"If there is one it will eat you first, Felix, and then I can run," she said when she was smaller, and I had to nod sagely and agree that was a very good idea.

"Lucy," I hissed into the dark. "Are you awake?"

There was nothing—apart from the foul odour I'd noticed earlier. My gaze cut to the window. It was shut.

I climbed out of bed and lit the candle on the nightstand, something I was only allowed to do in an emergency. I wandered around the nursery, my shadow following on the walls, trying to work out where the smell was coming from.

It was the farthest corner. Where the doll's house sat.

Tentatively, I opened the front, and the stench punched out. I gagged and stumbled backwards, holding my candle sconce aloft.

There was something in one of the bedrooms, laid upon a tiny bed.

I moved the candle closer, and the cry in my throat fluttered like a caged bird.

For there, on the pink and white checked coverlet, was the mouldering carcass of a mouse.

Only one person could have put it there. I glanced back to the sleeping form of my sister, the end of her thumb between her lips. Dread opened a cold fist in my gut.

Taking a muslin cloth from the chest of drawers, I scooped up the remains and tossed it out the window. It left a dark, wet stain upon the doll's bed.

In the morning I waited for Lucy to wake, having tossed and turned the whole night, but she didn't stir for all of my not so subtle whispering.

Eleanor came and went with her coal scuttle and still Lucy did not move.

Finally, I padded across to her bed and nudged her gently on the shoulder. Even through her nightgown her skin was burning hot, and my cry of alarm brought Eleanor racing back up the stairs.

By then I held Lucy in my arms, willing her closed eyes to open, trying to ignore the flushed pallor of her skin.

"You be going downstairs to fetch Hester," Eleanor said, her eyes wide with shock as she shooed me away.

The rest of the day passed in a blur of numb shock and doctor's visits. We were told to keep Lucy in bed until the fever passed, to open the windows for clean air, but it did little to ease the blanket of trepidation that had settled.

I was to keep away so she could rest, but I did steal back into the nursery a few times. At each visit my eyes were drawn to the doll resting in its white coffin, a mockery of Lucy tucked into her bed.

I took to wandering around the garden to get out of the house. When I could sleep, the strange bedroom with the vine-clad wallpaper—Mama had instructed I be moved—filled my dreams with rotting dolls dragged down into the earth.

On the afternoon of the third day, as I skimmed stones across the small pond at the back of the house, he came to me.

Dressed in the same raggedy clothes, Maverick Turner stood by the gate, his gaze fixed on the nursery window.

"I told you," he said. "No one ever believes me. I could smell the sickness on her."

Part of me wanted to charge at him and batter him senseless, even though I hadn't hit anything in my life, but the rush of burning heat that descended over my vision made me bold.

"No one can do that," I hissed at him. "Unless you're in league with the devil."

He looked me up and down, and I half expected an angry retort. "Do you want to save her?"

His words took all the breath from my lungs.

I would do anything to save her.

"You need to make Death think she's already been," he said, his eyes never leaving the window. "Your sister is marked, it's the only way."

I thought of how the doctor had dismissed Lucy's ailment as a chill, how even now he wasn't sure what afflicted her.

"Men of science." Maverick spat on the ground just as he had done outside the church. "They think they know everything."

"What do I have to do?"

"Surround her with dead things," he said, in a matter of fact way.

"How can I do that? They watch over her nearly all the time."

"You'll find a way." He paused, head cocked, as though he was listening to something. "Even laying them against her skin for a short time will help. And there's always…" he opened his mouth and stuck a finger under his tongue.

I recoiled in horror, and he frowned, shaking his head from side to side.

"You think you understand everything. But money can't buy what I know. Whether you do what I say, that's up to you, but if you don't…" he shrugged, turned on his heel, and in a few seconds was lost into the woods.

I wanted to run back into the house, forget any of this was happening, but his words had cut through me like a scythe. Against my better judgement I stole into the stables and scrabbled in the dusty chaff of the grain store. My fingers found the edge of what I was looking for. A vermin trap. The first two were empty, but the third contained the body of a plump rat. As I pulled back the spring mechanism surrounding its neck, bile rose in my throat, burning my tongue.

Its fur was still slightly warm, its black, beady eye open and bright. I stuffed it inside my jacket before I had a chance to hesitate. Then I ran back to the house, hoping no one would take any notice of the young master when the young mistress lay so still.

I made it to the nursery door.

"Felix." Mama was sitting in the far corner on the rocking chair, her form draped in shadow.

On her knee was the doll from the coffin.

A pungent aroma came from within the room, despite the lavender bags hanging from every surface.

The acrid scent of an illness reaching its peak.

My fingers closed over the bulge beneath my jacket.

"May I sit with her?"

Mama continued to rock for a few moments and then rose, letting the doll fall to the floor. The rustle of her skirts set my teeth on edge.

"Do not stay long," she whispered, her fingers trailing across my cheek. "Say what you have to say."

I knew then, knew from the tone of her voice and the way she had seemed to age a decade overnight, I knew that Lucy was dying.

I fell to my knees at her bedside and placed my hand over hers, so small and pale on the coverlet. I traced the rat's body along her arms, lifted the sheet and rubbed it against the soles of her feet.

She did not stir as I pleaded to whatever was out there for her survival.

It wasn't enough. I knew it wasn't enough.

What had Maverick said? I replayed his words, but one image stuck out, where he'd pointed under his tongue.

Maybe animals weren't enough. Maybe Death will only accept a human offering?

The thought, as it settled, made all the hair stand at the nape of my neck.

A breath of air left Lucy's lungs, the wheeze of it pained and putrid.

I kissed the back of her hand then fled, racing down the stairs as though the devil was on my heels. But he wasn't there, he was in my mind.

"Saddle my pony!" I screamed at the top of my lungs as I raced across the stable yard. I never gave orders, but right then, in that moment, I was master of this house and the groom obeyed without question. I was on Merlin's back in seconds, gathering the reins and putting my heels to his sides.

I crossed waterlogged fields and navigated a thick swathe of woodland. I paid no heed to the scratches on my face or the labouring of my mount.

I was off his back, stumbling to a dilapidated shack by a pig pen. I didn't knock but the door opened, and I nearly fell in.

Maverick stood in the doorway, his gaze wandering over my dishevelled state.

"I need more," I said.

"Can you pay?"

"I have coin." My hand fell to my pocket.

"Not that payment," Maverick replied and as his eyes met mine, I nodded.

Without another word he set off along the track and I followed, hardly able to comprehend what I was asking him or what I had agreed to.

As we came to a small clearing the birdsong that had accompanied us stopped. I followed his line of vision.

There, set in a row, were half a dozen mounds, roughhewn wooden markers at one end.

"Not everyone gets a silk-lined send off." He pulled a shovel from a tangle of gorse and pushed it into my hands. "Dig, rich boy."

I closed my fingers over the stout wood handle and despair took all my strength.

"Where?" It was the only word I could utter.

Maverick pointed to the nearest mound, freshly dug, the soil still dark and unmarked by grass or moss.

I dug as the afternoon light dwindled and the dark hovered. I dug even though blisters formed on my palms and my shirt stuck to my back with sweat. Every time I thought about stopping, I thought of Lucy.

The deeper I dug the more the stench grew. It crawled into my nostrils and traced its feelers down my throat. I threw up twice and Maverick simply watched.

I dug until my spade uncovered a rough length of cloth.

"Bring it here," he said, kneeling by the graveside.

I took hold of one end of the tied sack the body rested in and hauled it onto the forest floor.

It was a very small bundle.

"She died about a week ago." For the first time something like emotion showed on his face. "Fresh enough still to save your sister."

"I don't know what to do now." Helplessness made my hands shake.

He reached into his belt and pulled out a knife, handing it to me, hilt first.

"Take an eye. It's one of the last things to die."

I didn't ask how he knew.

My fingers tore at the sacking, and the exposed face struck terror into my heart. It was a young girl, her face bloated, blood-flecked foam leaking from her nostrils.

Maverick put his hand on my arm. "Quickly now."

I didn't hesitate, plunging the blade into the corner of one of the corpse's eyes. I felt the flesh collapse as I swept the edge behind the eyeball, severing all the vital threads of vision.

"Now," he said. "With your fingers, take it."

It was cold and glutinous on my palm like something from another world.

The butchered socket stared back at me, forlorn, empty.

"Go," he whispered, "I'll continue here. Put it under her tongue. But first," he paused, and his voice dropped an octave. "You must put it on yours, tell Death she has already called, to pass on by."

After what I had just done I had thought that nothing could shock me, but his words shook me to my core. Wrapping the eye in my handkerchief, I stumbled back along the track, ever-deepening gloom on my heels.

I don't remember the ride back home, but Merlin knew the way.

Now it is full dark and I sit by Lucy's bedside, a single candle lit on the nightstand, my handkerchief open on my palm.

The eye rests there, a glassy orb, severed threads trailing from it. My mouth feels like a cavern of dust.

I have to be quick. Mama hovers in the hallway, wringing her hands.

What if Maverick is wrong? What if he is playing the cruellest of tricks?

But, oh, what if he is telling the truth?

I gag as the eye touches my tongue, but I force it down somehow.

It tastes....bitter. Rancid. *Wrong*. But it's not the taste that heaves my stomach, it's the weight of it.

I swallow the saliva that has built in my mouth. I can feel the severed threads reaching down my throat as though they want to be a part of me.

I close my eyes, repeat the incantation I made up as I waited for Mama to let me enter.

This offering is death. You have called before. Move on now.

I say it seven times. It is Lucy's favourite number.

The eye sticks to my tongue as I remove it. It glistens with my saliva as I prise open my sister's lips. I try not to think of the little girl who died.

Of what I did to bring it here.

Lucy does not stir as I close her mouth. She does not know. For all of her fascination with death, it is better this way.

I want her to wake up screaming, to spit the eye out as Mama rushes into the room. I don't even care what they think of me, what they do to me.

I can still feel the weight of the eye on my tongue as I trudge down the darkened staircase to my bed.

Feet pounded up the stairs and dread clutched my heart. Stumbling out of bed I was met with Eleanor. She grabbed my shoulders and swung me around, the social standing between us lost in the elation.

"Miss Lucy, Master Felix. She's awake. Heaven be praised!"

Lucy was sitting in bed. Her nightgown freshly pressed, her hair shining and done up with ribbons, her skin glowing with health.

I waited until Mama had gone, then sat on the edge of the bed and took Lucy's hand.

"What dreams I had, Felix," she said, her eyes wide and solemn. "I dreamt I was dead and buried under the earth then someone dug me up and…" she paused, her hand rising to rub her eye.

I looked away, palms sweating.

"There was an awful taste in my mouth, too. And something like Cook's disgusting aspic jelly on my tongue."

I didn't have the right words to reply.

"Do you want your doll?"

Lucy shook her head. "I don't want to play at dead things anymore, Felix."

I heard later that Maverick had been caught by the child's grave. They thought he was desecrating it. There was only one way it would end for him now.

Maybe I should have spoken up, confessed my part in the sin, but they wouldn't have believed me. Lucy would know what I had done and she would never look at me the same way again.

I returned to my privileged life, but what I did is an ever-present stain on my soul.

Lucy is a young woman now, the belle of society, suitors queuing at the doors. Mama succumbed to a fever two years past, and now I am the master of Ellerby Hall.

The hour is late, and I've retired to my study. The walls are covered with bookshelves but by the window there is a tall cupboard with a padlock. The key I keep with me always.

Inside the cupboard are rows of glass jars. Inside the jars, covered in preserving liquid, are my treasures. The rich can acquire anything with the proper contacts.

I do not think about the midnight graveyards and the plundered graves, the lanterns held aloft in the misty dark, the mutilated skulls of the newly dead.

Sometimes I think I can smell Death waiting.

"Can you pay?"

I open a jar, scoop out the contents and rinse it in the bowl of water on the sill. I am fixated. Tormented. Bewitched.

Need opens a hand, and I cannot resist.

Moonlight streams through the window as I place it on my tongue. The weight of it instantly soothes my nerves even as my stomach heaves. I find it both repulsive and compelling.

Do I have to continue with this macabre ritual? Probably not. Lucy is safe. But I crave it.

I pluck the eye from my mouth, add it to the tumbler of brandy by my side. It watches me from the bottom of the glass. Is there an accusation there? I drain all the contents in one long swallow. Don't judge me for what you do not understand.

The sound of Lucy's laughter echoes from the drawing room and all is well.

3:00 MEATING

by Chad Lutzke

Juicy and I were talking about the weather, when a man pulled away from pump three without paying. Happened at least once a month there at Fast Filler Gas Station. We didn't run after him, didn't even move, just made note of the license plate, wrote it on a piece of paper, and taped it to the side of the register.

"Guess I'll get outta your hair, let you make the call," I told him.

He'd just started his shift. Mine had just ended. Sometimes I was envious, him working first. Then I'm reminded how much I don't care for people these days, and third shift suits me best. It's quiet. Not a lot of customers.

Took me about five minutes to get home. Mr. Lambert was out jogging, and he offered a wave. I didn't used to like the man, thought he was some kind of pervert. I can't imagine why else you'd want to be a gynecologist. He also coached girls' volleyball over at Springview High. These were red flags. But, when my wife left me for another man, Mr. Lambert was the one who caught her. He came right to me, filled me in. That's when I realized the child she was carrying wasn't even mine. My heart split in two, and for the next three weeks, Mr. Lambert came over every day to check on me. On the weekends he'd even bring a six pack, and we'd watch Norris and Stallone flicks. Turns out, he's not so bad after all, even if he does stare at cooch nine to five.

I toasted four Pop-Tarts and downed a glass of orange juice while an old movie played in the background. Per routine, I drifted off, until the phone woke me an hour before the alarm would. It was Colette. My ex.

"Gary. Sorry if I woke you. Did I wake you?"

"You're fine," I told her.

"Okay. Well…we need food."

"Again?"

The phone crackled with a heavy sigh. "We've had a bad month, Gary. First, Timothy fell off his bike, had to get four stiches on his forehead. Then he had a field trip, and I had to spring for that, and then he needed new school shoes…"

Congratulations, you're being a parent. It's what they do, I thought.

"It's just been one thing after another," she continued.

Finally, the spiel ended, and an awkward silence took over, as she waited for me to tell her not to worry, I'd buy some groceries. What I wanted to say was, "Tough shit. This ain't even my kid. And if you were any kind of a decent woman his dad would still be around." But I'm predictable and had her give me a list, told her I'd stop by before work, then hung up without another word.

When I showed up to work at eleven p.m., Juicy was still there, worked a double. Someone had called in. He counted his drawer, and I scooted him outta there. The poor guy had to clock back in at seven a.m.

I filled the coffee pots, swept, and grabbed my paperback while I waited for a customer. Except for a small rush after the bars close, on average I'd get about eight an hour until around three, then maybe one every hour. It makes for plenty of reading time. When I tire of that, I go outside and stretch my legs, gaze at the stars if they're out, and ponder my existence. That's what I was doing when I saw the figure in the playground across the street.

Its gait was broken, almost shambling across the freshly cut grass and toward the slide, where it bent over and placed something on it. Something that shined in the moonlight. Something that *glistened.* Even as I squinted, I couldn't make it out. Then the figure turned and shambled back across the lot and off into the trees.

If this were anything but a playground, I would have ignored my curiosity, but children would be on those grounds in a matter of hours—Colette's kid. Juicy's kid. And if some deranged homeless sadomasochist left something there to harm them, I needed to know. Drugs, dirty needles, feces. A number of things crossed my mind.

Completely preoccupied with the mystery, I waited impatiently for a customer to show, meeting the anticipated hourly quota, then locked the door, crossed the street, and ran to the slide.

I got about ten feet from it before realizing what it was. Someone had left a raw slab of raw meat at the bottom of the slide, covered in bits of grass and dirt as though it'd been dropped.

I looked toward the woods. If anyone was standing there, they were lost in the shadows. There could have been a whole village of people watching me and I wouldn't have seen a thing.

I kicked the meat from the slide and pulled a rag from my pocket, wiped the slide down, doing my best to rid it of any blood. Then, I wrapped the rag around my hand, grabbed the meat, and high-tailed it back to work.

I tossed the thing in the dumpster, unlocked the door, and headed inside to wash my hands. I spent the next few minutes debating whether to call the police. I thought of the time I called after seeing a boy letting air out of a tire in the IHOP parking lot. The cops belittled me. They had better things to do, places to be. I decided this would be more of the same so spent the rest of the night watching the playground, hoping the figure would come again.

When Juicy showed up for work, I told him what happened.

"You think it was a practical joke?" he said.

"Could be. But what's the joke?"

"Not a very good one. Dog shit I could understand. A steak? Not so much."

"Even if it was a joke," I said. "This was an adult…like an old man."

"Probably homeless. Maybe he was gonna come back for it, cook it over a fire, and you went and grabbed the best meal he's had in weeks."

It was a theory. But not one I put much faith in. Not the way he'd laid it down and gone off. He wasn't coming back. He'd done what he set out to do.

I slept sound throughout the day, then heated up some Salisbury and tater tots, plopped in front of the TV and flipped through the channels, settling on *Columbo*. I was feeling nostalgic. In the episode, Columbo was on a stakeout, using binoculars. I started thinking about the slab of meat I'd found and wondered if the person would show again. I decided I'd have my own little stakeout, right there from the gas station

When I got to work, Shawna was there, the manager. She said she wasn't sure Juicy would be there in the morning, something about his kid being pretty shook up about an event at school. No other details.

She left, and I spent some time arranging the few shelves we had, filled with everything from motor oil to snack cakes and even a box of those little rubber monsters kids put on the ends of their fingers, with the tiny arms dangling and shaking with seizure-like motion. I'd tried to get Shawna to replace some of the bullshit with items that'd bring customers in, but she was stubborn as a splinter.

Except for a drunk woman who asked to use the restroom, then left with the entire roll of toilet paper hidden under her shirt, the evening was uneventful. Until three a.m. That's when I saw the figure again.

I grabbed the binoculars. The darkness hindered any detail, but I managed to see it was a man, his face covered in silver hair. And just like the night before, he carried something with him in a grocery bag.

I watched him empty the bag onto the slide, then look around like I'd seen so many kids do right before they swiped a chocolate bar from the shelf. The man did not want to get caught. Then he turned and walked back toward the woods, brisker than before. I watched until he was out of sight, then I focused on the slide, but through the dim scope of the binoculars, I couldn't make out what he'd left behind. So, I locked the store and ran across the street. The playground was basked in the usual dull, streetlight glow, with little help from the moon, just enough to add a sparkle to the steel slide ahead. As I drew closer, I could see the four stiff legs of a cat. It's orange and white fur crusted brick-red and matted from a roadside grave bed. A far worse prank to confuse and traumatize the kids but equally as bizarre.

I quickly grabbed it by the tail, but the fur came off in my hand and the tiny corpse fell to the ground, raising a small cloud of dirt at the bottom of the slide, where hundreds of children's feet landed five days a week. I snatched the thing again, taking no time to be careful.

"Sorry," I found myself saying as I ran with the cat swinging by my side, stuck in a permanent death coil, one side flat as though it'd melted on brutally hot pavement earlier that late-summer day.

I set it *behind* the dumpster and not *in* it. I envisioned a heartbroken owner hanging posters on nearby telephone poles, coming into the station to ask if I'd seen their lost tabby, then my response of having heartlessly thrown the beloved thing in the trash. If possible, I'd rather return the body to its grieving owner–no matter how mangled–so they could provide a proper burial.

I unlocked the store, jumped back into my paperback and read through a thick distraction, my mind preoccupied with why in the hell someone would continually prank innocent children with raw meat and a dead cat. How long had this been going on?

I was eager to share it all with Juicy and ask if he'd seen the man, but the clock hands on the wall were snails on a disc of honey, the next several hours going by like a right hook in an underwater dream.

Juicy showed up a half an hour early. I told him about the cat, then asked about his son.

Juicy shook his head with disbelief. "He's fine now but had quite a scare. One of his classmates was running during recess, didn't see the swing set and cracked his shin right in half against the bar. Bone and everything. Hell on the kid, of course, but pretty traumatic for the students. Shook my boy up pretty good."

I wondered if Colette's boy had seen it too. "Damn! They won't forget that."

"No, they won't. And they wouldn't forget a dead cat on the slide either. Good on you for taking care of it."

"I'm staking the playground out tonight."

Juicy tapped a smoke from a pack he pulled out of his shirt pocket and lit it. "You don't work tonight, do ya?"

"No, but I don't have anything better to do, so it's either get to the bottom of this guy's kink or watch the same movies all night."

"Thought you were a reader."

"I can read in the car, with one eye on the playground."

"I can do the same, ya know. Right here at the store." Juicy blew smoke out the side of his mouth.

"No. I want to do it. But this time, I'm intervening. And if I have to, I'll send a message not to do it again."

"You seem a little…obsessed. It's not like he's out there roughing kids up, looking up dresses."

"For all we know, he's standing in the woods beating his meat while they're out playing."

"No pun intended?" Juicy chuckled.

"I'm serious," I said.

"Maybe calling the police is a better idea. You sound like you're ready to start swingin' if you see the guy again."

"If it stops him from leaving dead animals for the kids to find, well…"

"Shit, Gary…you serious?"

It was a good question.

Once I got home, it took me nearly two hours to get to sleep. My mind was preoccupied, searching for reason. What's this guy's purpose? Is this the beginning of something worse? Like a serial killer who begins his penchant for death with animals, until his blood lust can no longer be satiated and moves onto humans. Onto children.

I decided if I saw him again, I would go to the police. If this really was the beginning of something worse, he needed to know more than just a gas station clerk was onto him.

When I finally crashed, I dreamt of kids covered in blood. Little girls with bare legs covered in tacky crimson, hair matted with rust, permanently wide eyes and slack jaws. Prepubescent screams that echoed for years.

I had to stop him.

By midnight, I was on my way. I brought the binoculars, a pizza, a few bottles of water, and my paperback. But I never read a word. My eyes were glued to the slide. I was afraid to even blink.

I parked the car away from any streetlight, then scanned the playground, making sure he hadn't already paid a visit. The sky was overcast, threatening rain. I wasn't worried about getting wet, but I was afraid it'd keep the mystery man at bay. And if I'm being honest, I wanted him to show. I needed that push over the edge to both confront him and contact the police. If I even called them. My fists and a baseball bat could do more than any man in blue.

According to the last two nights, three a.m. was his hour of arrival, and as the time drew closer, my stomach filled with lava, my eyes dry and sore from gazing, gazing, gazing with violent determination.

This break in the monotony of my everyday routine was surreal. I was on a stakeout, waiting hours for a stranger to partake in his own routine–a sick ritual no number of hours of contemplation would ever reveal a potential for, and the more I thought on it, the more I had to know. Juicy was right. I had become obsessed.

I pictured children sprinting from the brick schoolhouse as the recess bell rang, each of their faces split wide with toothy smiles, racing to be the first on the merry-go-round, the first to the swings.

The first to the slide.

Where they would cast themselves down blindly into a bloody carcass, staining their clothes and scarring their naive minds with images of bellies split wide and teeming with maggots, bulging eyes, loose tongues, and crooked teeth. Even the slab of raw meat from a butcher shop was enough to send shivers up the spines of the innocent, as it sat there out of context like a drop of ink on a wedding dress, its glistening marbled swirls and spongy give atop the star-shine metal of their playground toy.

Just a few minutes after three, the black line of trees parted, and the figure poured forth, shambling more than usual. As I pulled the binoculars to my eyes, I saw why. This time the bag he carried was canvas, which dragged behind him. This was no slab of steak or single cat.

I got out of the car, quietly, bringing with me a baseball bat. I dodged the light and stuck with shadows until I reached a tree wide enough to hide behind. At this point, the man was no more than twenty feet in front of me. There was still no telling what was in the bag, but it seemed heavy enough to hold a large dog. Or a child.

Not once did the man turn, his eyes fixed on the destination ahead. The slide. I stayed behind the tree, waiting for him to reveal the contents of the bag, praying to God it wasn't human.

He stopped, stretched his arm and rubbed his shoulder, arched his back, then shuffled the remaining few yards to the slide, where he scanned the playground. I pulled my peering face back behind the tree and waited a moment, then peeked again. He was holding the bottom of the canvas bag, struggling to empty it. Finally, I saw the contents inside. It *was* a dog. I breathed a sigh of relief and watched as the man grabbed the poor thing's front end and lift it, resting its head on the end of the slide, while its stiff legs remained straight as though frozen.

I'd seen enough. With the bat by my side, I walked toward the man, who must have heard me coming because he turned, much quicker than I thought him capable of. His hair was peppered gray and shaggy, poking out from under an old baseball cap. His jeans had a hole in the knee revealing dirty, scabbed skin, and his face wore deep, troubled lines with purple bags under ice-blue eyes that hung like two leeches spooning the orbs. I guessed his age at about sixty-five, but his gait was of someone at least twenty years older.

He gave an agitated sigh when he saw me, then grabbed the cap on his head and ran a forearm across the dirty gray shag.

"What the hell you doing, old man?" I said.

"Mind your business, son. I ain't hurtin' nobody."

"Ain't hurting nobody?" I was shocked by his response, the articulation of it, the calm voice, free of slur or stumbling embarrassment.

He put his cap back on. "Trust me. They'll never see it."

"Yeah, thanks to me. For three nights now I've seen you out here dumping shit on this slide."

He chuckled, rubbed at his shoulder. "Three nights, eh? Son, I been doing this every night for the last ten years…three thousand, four-hundred-and-ninety-eight days to be exact."

I called bullshit and told him I'd been working at the gas station for nearly that long. I would have seen him.

"Ain't as spry as I used to be. Not surprised you caught me. Not too long ago I could get in and out of here without so much as the moonlight spotting me. These days, not so much. You made good timing, I suppose. And now it's time to pass the torch."

I'd had a few days to deal with the shock of seeing a grown man drop a dead cat (and raw beef) at an elementary school playground, but now there was something new I wasn't prepared for. His demeanor. Every word he said felt honest, genuine. There was no sense of shame or embarrassment for being caught.

I struggled to find my next words. Only a minute ago I was ready to escort this man off the grounds using whatever force necessary, but now stood dumbfounded. I'd found myself in the strangest conversation I'd ever had.

I went back to my original question. "What in the hell are you doing out here?"

"You ain't left me no choice but to tell you. I'm being forced into this." Then he shouted his next few words as though they weren't meant for me but someone else in the distance. "You hear that!? I've been forced to pass the torch!"

I looked down at the poor Golden Retriever with its tongue touching metal, its hair healthy and shifting against a subtle breeze. The sight brought me back to the ire I felt when I first grabbed the bat. "You got about thirty seconds to tell me why you're doing this, then leave, and never come back."

The old man looked straight into my eyes. They were kind, trustworthy, filled with concern, but not for himself. "You need to listen to me. I'm going to tell you this one time, then I'm leaving. And I'm *not* coming back. Not ever. This is your problem now." He seemed to give me a moment before carrying on. "This poor critter here..." He pointed to the dog, and his chin quivered as though he might cry. "He's an offering. Without the offering, a kid gets hurt. Sometimes worse."

I gave the man a little shove with the bat. "Get the hell outta here. And just so you know, I'm not the only one who'll be watching this playground. I'm calling the po–"

"I told you, boy...you need to listen. If you don't show up here around three tomorrow with an offering, you're putting a kid's life in danger. This goes back well before you were born. Hell, before I was born. Not just here but other schools. And before you ask what it is, I can't tell you. It ain't beast nor man nor demon nor ghost. Is it of this world? I've speculated and came to the conclusion it is not. But it's got a deviant hunger, and it don't ever show itself."

I cracked a smile more from repulsion than finding any humor in his words. "You're trying to tell me you're out here feeding some evil entity nobody can see because if it doesn't get what it wants it kills kids?"

"I don't expect you to believe it. I didn't. Until a child died after I refused to comply. Coincidence? Maybe. But I wasn't willing to take the chance."

This time the smile I wore was a snarky one, as I'd already destroyed the madman's theory without him knowing. "You know...the last two nights, I've taken your *offering*."

The man's eyes grew wide as saucers. "You took them?"

"Yep...and not a thing happened."

The man slumped to the ground, like the life had been sucked out of him, and sat, staring off. "You don't know that for sure."

"I'm pretty sure I'd know."

He put a hand to his face, and his eyes went glassy with tears. "Aww hell, son…It ain't right in your face. A kid dies, you might never know. Sometimes they don't die at all. Sometimes they just get hurt, real bad."

I was going to come at him with more rebuttal, when I remembered Juicy's son's classmate. "Do they only get hurt on the playground?"

"Couldn't tell you. It took one death for me to show up here every night at three a.m. and leave what I could, so I'd like to think I've stopped anything bad from happening since. But I've heard stories."

"From who?"

"The one who carried the torch before me. He ain't around no more. He said the hurt wasn't always physical, sometimes psychological. Scars that run deep. He said those were like threats that shit would get worse. He called it malevolent grace. Any time there wasn't a death, it was some kinda twisted pardon. But after that…death loomed."

Kids get hurt on playgrounds every day. Juicy's kid's classmate was no different. I was done listening to the drivel.

"Get the fuck outta here," I said.

He stood, brushed himself off, threw his hands in the air as a sign of surrender. "I'm gone…but you need to leave tonight's offering be, especially since you've taken the last few. Then you need to bring another tomorrow, and the day after that. Once you're caught by peering eyes, you spill the curse onto the next. But make damn sure it's to someone who'll play their part."

"I've heard enough bullshit, old man. I see you again, it won't end well."

He started walking away but kept talking. "Animals appease the beast. A few nights a week you can get away with a fat steak, but you try and pull that every night, it won't go well for the innocent."

It was the last thing he said before disappearing into the trees, leaving me with the canvas bag and the dead retriever.

I watched the tree line like a kid does a darkened staircase, imagining the horror of seeing a ghostly figure appear. Nothing came.

I dragged the dog to the gas station and left it behind the dumpster with the cat. I'd give them another day and if nobody asked around for missing pets, I'd have to toss them. Before heading home, I stopped in the station, paid a quick visit to the weekend shift, and grabbed a soda. It was after four a.m. when I got home.

I have to admit, I had a hint of curiosity at what I'd been told. The world is full of unknowns, surely some lay hidden for only a select few to find. And who would believe the discoverers? These secrets kept secure even when spilled. You'd be declared insane. A charlatan.

What had happened to the boy on the playground just two days before, after I'd taken the "offering," was disconcerting. And what if the trauma of seeing your peer writhe in the gravelly sand, bone jutting through ripped flesh, was another form of this wicked price to pay?

...sometimes psychological. Scars that run deep.

But what of coincidence? That too exists. A school playground is nothing more than a plot filled with careless cavorting. Sprained ankles, splinters, skinned knees, and bruised ankles galore, some worse than others. Like fractured limbs.

But according to the old man, punishment wasn't always dealt on school grounds.

I couldn't entertain the nonsense any longer. Simply put, the man had a unique case of OCD, where he'd given into an odd compulsion in order to keep at bay the idea something bad may happen should he not perform his ritual, though taking it even farther and creating his own lore behind it. Whether that lore stemmed from a delusional state, or he was simply a liar, I wasn't sure.

Yet I spent the next three hours in sickly rumination, followed by more dreams of blood-covered children, pink ribbons tangled in matted hair. Skinless, limbless, pulsating masses of flesh that moaned my name through lipless mouths, begging me to be their savior.

I showed up at work after Juicy had started his shift. I had to tell him everything I knew.

"Behind the dumpster?" Juicy said in between customers.

"If nobody asks by tonight I'll toss 'em in."

"That's fuckin' weird...I mean, the old man."

"What do you make of it?" I asked.

"What's there to make of it? The guy's fuckin' nuts."

Juicy helped confirm the ridiculousness of it. And it didn't take long before I felt like an idiot for wasting a single thought on any truth behind the man's insane declaration.

Then I heard sirens, which halted nearby. I looked through the gas-station windows and saw a convoy of emergency responders pull into the school. Before I knew it, I was already across the street, racing toward a crowd of people near the monkey bars. People had gathered like ants around melting candy. I beat the paramedics to the scene and squeezed through. I had to see.

In the middle of the crowd was Colette's son, with his teeth through his tongue, his neck impossibly twisted. He was still.

I barely knew him. To him, I was nothing more than an estranged uncle who showed up when times got tough for his mom. He had no idea the history between his mother and I, or his long-gone, home-wrecking father. But his small lifeless body shook me.

It took one death for me to show up here every night at three a.m.…

Children were sobbing, hyperventilating, clutching the legs of teachers.

A compound fracture and a broken neck in the same week. Suddenly, sanity became an deceiving fiend, and lunacy the only safe place to hide.

Later, through the first four hours of my shift, my eyes were drawn to that thick black line on the other side of the playground–a void holding secrets? Or merely a haven for pre-teen adventure filled with climbable limbs?

I watched the ebony curtain like it was the mouth of the devil himself, waiting to open wide for its three-a.m. meal.

…you need to leave tonight's offering…Then you need to bring another tomorrow, and the day after that.

Was I adopting someone else's obsessiveness like some psychosomatic contagion? As I amused the voice of reason, I knew deep down how the night would end. The haunting "what-ifs" were too strong to ignore.

Just before three a.m., I locked up the station and went out back, behind the dumpster. I grabbed the stuffed canvas bag and carried the reeking retriever across the street. I had the cat still. I would use it tomorrow.

After that, things would get difficult.

A dog barked in the distance, and I wondered if he could see the unseeable thing in the woods, alarming me to its presence. I wondered if he smelled the danger like the onset of cancer. I wondered how bad his owner will miss him.

SKIN MAPS

by Shane Hawk

"No, fucker. Remember the official report on that Switzerland particle collider? They discovered dimensions beyond our own after creating those microscopic black holes," Sequoyah says, eyeing me from all the way up on his high horse, orange spirits glistering in his pupils.

"I'll show you a microscopic black hole," I say, swigging the last of my warmed beer. Instinctively, I reach for another cig from my jean jacket's breast pocket. Stretching the pack his way and nodding my chin at it, I offer Sequoyah one, too.

"I'm good. Got my juicer, anyway. If I'mma fuck up my lungs, I'll do it with tech from this century, not those vintage-ass cancer sticks," he says, waving his hacked device burning capsules of whatever banned drug you could want.

After rolling my eyes and pocketing my pack again, I lean forward to place another log into the crepitating campfire. Its heat licks my fingertips and crawls up my arm. The other smoldering logs shift, causing the flames to rise and shoot off tiny embers that die in the wind. The stars are legion, as if thousands of warriors took aim at the black mass and shot holes into it.

"So, you think we can peer into the in-between worlds—like liminal spaces?" I ask.

Sequoyah belches and the godawful stench of half-digested summer sausage and spiced rum violates my nostrils. "You really don't remember those news reports? Man, they could straight up disclose the existence of aliens, and no one would care, at least the sheep. Would just be a Comm notification to be swiped away." He laughs at his observation, giving himself more credit than he deserves. "Not just *peer into* them. Fuckin' EarthGov has been experimenting with travel using them shits. Like super-speed doorways that catapult you the fuck across space. And? We Ordinaries can visit these doorways." Sequoyah says, polishing off his beer to catch up with me.

"Visit them how?"

"Shit, if you'd finally indulge in some drugs with me, you'd find out."

"You know, it's hard for me to trust others, especially when drugs are involved. You know, the farm."

"Can't even stomach what they did to you. And they called themselves Christians. But it's just me, oginalii. You know I'd make it safe for you. Trust."

"Let's say I give in and smoke something with you. How the fuck does that open a black hole, Quo? Come on, man."

"Not exactly. But I've got my hands on some old-school DMT."

"Isn't that the shit stoners used to call the 'Spirit Molecule'?" I ask.

"For a reason," Quo says.

At this, I'm standing and stretching my arms, cracking my back to gesture that I'm tired and barely interested in his drugs and global conspiracies. "And how do you know all this, Quo? You're just an Indian—an Ordinary—out here under the same stars as me."

"I got my sources, cabrón. No te preocupes," Quo says, smiling like a madman before he rips an impressive hit from his juicer.

For a moment, I study Quo, appreciating my zany Cherokee and Mexican friend I met while working the late shifts at a chemical plant years ago—the one we both got fired from for undermining their mission. He's gaunt from off-grid living, his angular facial features and squinty eyes giving him counterfeit pensiveness. Just like any other day, his attire comprises a blank tee covered by an open flannel, jeans, and dark brown boots. Over his sable hair that damn near reaches his nuts, he's sporting an orange beanie with embroidery that reads, LANDBACK, BITCH. The funny thing is people like him, those who appear non compos, get things done. Despite the tribes of the Northwestern Continent reclaiming great deals of their land, there's still a plethora being held by the EarthGov. It's the war that never ceases, but to be honest, would we sign yet another underhanded treaty? Hell, we were lucky legislation like the historical ICWA got reinstated after losing it some twenty years ago—back when this landmass was still called the United States. Well, I wasn't lucky in that regard. My foster family and that GMO farm…

I crouch to lie down on my blanket and take in the stars. "Not worried, hermano. Just tired, sorry." While Quo shifts around to stargaze with me, I'm itching my knees I scraped when shooting hoops last week. Doing my best Phil Jordon impression, I drank a bit too much before our game, and the other team schooled us. Extensive, gnarled scabs cover both my legs from knee to shin.

"Fool, don't pick at your scabs. Didn't your mom ever—" Quo catches himself and muzzles his role as deprecator.

Before he can sit up and spit out his apology, I hit him with a: "It's okay, brother. I'm past all that," deterrent. But really, I'm staring at the endless orbs above, wondering whether my parents' souls are blinking back at me.

Mom and Dad died before I could walk. Authorities placed me in the ProviDoor Program—a public-private entity "providing opportunities by opening doors for today's youth"—under the care of impassive NonNates who owned one too many acres of farmland. No memory of my parents or family. Didn't know them. Still don't know my tribes. And I've spent many a night like this, silently suffering underneath the vast weight of the ever-expanding universe. It keeps growing while I feel smaller each day. Will life get better?

"No, really, man. It shouldn't have slipped," Quo says, his hand rubbing the back of his neck, causing his face to strain. "Love you, Daniel. You been through so much. Here for you, always."

Daniel. Was that even my birth name? Throughout the years, I've pretended to have different names from different tribes, as if a name could change who I am or how I feel. "Love you, too, Sequoyah. I know you mean it. Think it's time for lights out," I say before I smother the fire with handfuls of earth.

The shard of moon hanging in the sky gives off just enough silvery light to illumine the pillar of smoke ascending to the cosmos. Despite the elite members of the Global High Society slowly ruining this planet, it's still beautiful. I'm unsure they could really take that away from us, but damn if they aren't determined.

Quo and his drug pitch swirl through my bloodstream, permeating my blood-brain barrier and nuzzling into the gummy crevices of my mind. Is that pineal gland bullshit real? I focus on the supposed "doorways" and wonder if it's worth a shot.

"Quo?" I say.

"Yeah, bro, still awake."

"I'm down."

"Really now?" Quo says. Though it's dark, I know the left corner of his mouth is raising with his eyebrows. As if reading my thoughts, he snaps on a halogen, and we both sit up to face each other. "Skoden, broden."

"Did you really just—"

"Man, shut the fuck up and take this first," Quo says, passing me a piece of paper.

"Is this a tab of acid?"

"Nah, not LSD, but similar. A bit punchier. In your fancy educated talk, I'd say it's a 'prerequisite' for the journey you're about to take."

"You're not doing it with me?" I ask. Twisting the small scrap of paper in my hand back and forth, I can't discern any perceivable characteristics. I raise it to my nose. "Smells like sour candy," I say.

"I'mma sit this one out so I can be here for your safety. Don't worry." Quo giggles incessantly as if he's pranking me, then says, "Bro, I know you gotta sweet tooth. That's why I asked for this flavor. For this very moment. Just fold it once, put it under your tongue, and keep your mouth closed."

I do exactly what he instructs me to do because I can't risk fucking up my first foray into Drugland. Plus, he's got all the experience in the world.

Demons of the underworld are fighting to pull my eyelids down with all their might. Lethargy is seeping into my veins like oil into brackish waters, and Sequoyah's voice is muffled, as if I'm drowning in those very waters, and he's shouting just above me from a lake dock. Am I still sitting before Quo? He's fading from sight, as are the halogen lamp and our campsite. Squinting my eyes, I strain to see anything distinguishable. Only irradiant flashes, like lightning, and clouds filter past me. The sensory input overwhelms and sends my anxiety to dreadful levels.

I just want to shut my fucking eyes!

As I reopen, my retinas process a tranquil meadow at high noon, and I take in a noiseless gasp. Distant birdsong, the drone of bees, and rustling branches fill my ears. I can even smell berries as the sun warms my skin. Hummingbirds approach a flowering tree for nectar, whitetail deer lap up a creek, and cottontails feast on dandelions. How long ago is this? The whitetail went extinct before I was born… Something tickles my outer wrist, and as I pull it toward me, a common house ant makes its way to my hand, treading around to my palm.

But there's something off about it. The ant is walking backward.

Raising my head to view the meadow once again, I witness all the creatures' backward, distorted movements, as if they're glitching. My right hand is ablaze with pain and my eyes track down to glimpse the tiny ant has morphed into a carpenter ant as it burrows into my palm, fiery blood melting down my forearm. I shake my arm in a vain attempt to rid myself of the large ant's grip, but its stinging fangs are crunching into my tendons.

A guttural yell gushes up my throat from the pit in my stomach. The animals remain unphased and can't hear me; their backward movements are still rigid and robotic. My instinct is to scream, flail my arms, and run around, but my feet are immovable, like in a bad dream. My entire right leg is consumed by crackling carpenter ants. They trail up my torso, down my arm, and into my hand hole. So many ants are biting that my hand is now splitting down the middle, rending into two halves. The blistering pain is more than flesh and blood can stand.

I clench my eyes and grit my teeth, wishing for it all to go away.

My breathing slows as I center my thoughts. A new scene slowly reveals itself as I inch my eyes open again. I'm soaring like a crow above what used to be South Dakota. Black Elk Peak is recognizable, as I've hiked that trail three times and back. And the Black Hills… no ugly presidents are carved into its granite.

By now, I'm floating over Rapid City, but it isn't as conspicuous as it should be. Instead, clusters of dwellings dot the area with no visible streets or prison-like American suburbia patterns. There's no major roadway where Interstate 90 used to be.

I sail above the Great Plains for a while before observing thousands of bison migrate toward a valley, the luscious blue-green Missouri River pumping through like a healthy vein. Everything is so green, so beautiful. There doesn't seem to be any visible damage from oil companies, corporate farms, or hyper-consumerism.

Did I already enter through one of Quo's doorways? I don't remember him mentioning alternate universes unless that's what he meant by extra dimensions. Though the sights are calming, my heartbeat multiplies, and I wonder how long drug trips are supposed to last. Feels like I've been tripping for hours.

Brooding clouds and lightning strikes return. I have to close my eyes again because of the sheer speed of the wind. The roaring and whistling gusts remind me of the tornados I'd survived at the farm. Malevolent devastators trying to wipe you from the face of the earth, angry that we hid in those shelters.

The rumbling wind abates, and I catch my breath while thick blood pumps through my ears and neck.

"Are you going to just sit there with closed eyes, or will you show me respect during your visit?" a quavery voice asks.

As my shoulders tighten and my lips tremble, I crack my eyes open to peek at who's speaking to me. The shaky voice belongs to an elderly woman, maybe in her nineties, with a dark complexion, save for the liver spots blanketing her hands and arms. In defiance of her manifest age, her hair is a distinct salt and pepper and a purple shawl drapes her shoulders. Her eyes hide behind black sunglasses, and she's wearing a denim blouse, a pink handkerchief with geometric patterns hanging from its left pocket.

"Who—"

"You know who I am, boy," she says, her lips pursing and eyebrows raising from behind her dark shades. "Search within yourself."

"Are you my grandma?" I ask, swallowing over three decades of curiosity and loneliness.

"It's not for me to say. This is clearly your peregrination. What answers do you truly seek?" The elderly woman is pushing her lips and chin up, running her tongue along her teeth, or lack thereof. As she finishes, her salient feature is now her mouth of decay, a melange of yellowed and blackened teeth.

"To whom do I belong? To where do I belong?" I ask, a frog of fear leaping and occluding my airway. My stomach knots and folds in on itself; my mouth becomes dry.

"Is this your crowning moment? Will the answers to these questions rectify your lifelong spirit of inquiry?"

"Spirit of inquiry? What do you—"

"Hush, child. Do not harbor reservations about my methods. It's a yes or a no."

"Yes," I say, biting my bottom lip and lowering my eyes to her swollen ankles. Diabetes?

"Look beneath your skin, and your lineage and homeland will be unveiled."

"My skin?" I ask, discomposure coating my voice.

"Peel it off," she spits back. Her voice shifting to a masculine, boisterous tone catches me off guard, causing black ice to rip through my spinal column. My eyes rise from her handkerchief to meet hers as she removes her sunshades.

Her eyes are… hollow. Mere windows with the starry sky behind them.

"Peel off your skin if you want to know!" she barks, and a black carpenter ant flings out of her gaping maw, hitting my chest. I flick the ant, and out of my periphery, I glimpse an army of fluttering winged ants ripping my hand apart.

My raging scream emits no sound.

As my gaze returns to the Elder, a torrent of winged swarmer ants burst out of her eyes in all directions and encircles us. The menacing hive hisses and forms a Stygian specter ready to strike and devour us, leaving nothing but pocked, yellowed bones. A few carpenters barge their way into my ear canals and nostrils, their wings and legs wriggling against the walls of my orifices. I'm shaking my head and shrieking, to no avail.

"Look beneath… your… skin," the booming, demonic voice croaks.

And all at once, the floor beneath me disappears and gravity tugs me downward, my limbs swimming slowly as if filled with lead. I'm in outer space, flickering stars and blackness engulfing my body. The old woman has vanished, along with her horde of ants.

Debris and gases swirl to form images to my left and right.

On my left, my mind is projecting a memory from the farm when I angered my foster dad, Paul, by questioning his use of certain pesticides and seeds. I'm watching my own memory on playback as he's strapping me down in the barn, shoving pills into my mouth, forcing me to ingest them all. He liked to twist his empty beer cans, creating a saw-toothed edge, and scrape them against my legs. Never knew if his wife was aware or approved, but she wasn't much better.

Wincing away to my right, I gape at a high school memory. White parents influenced their kids to hate us Natives just as much as them on account so many tribes had regained stewardship of their homelands and water sources around that time. This memory playing on a backdrop of space dust is from when the basketball captain and other teammates took me behind the gym after school. They only let me on the team because I was tall for my age and could defend the ball. The previous week, I purposely underperformed because my entire class mocked Natives at the pep rally. The student emcee had the entire gymnasium put one hand behind their head to simulate feathers, and with the other hand, cup it to their howling mouths to mimic a war cry. I'm reliving the captain brandishing a fixed blade and holding it parallel to my face, the blade's edge threatening to puncture my skin. He's sobbing the usual, banal white anger stuff I've heard all my life, like, "You lost. This is our land now, savage. Y'all should've died in the Old West." A school security guard yells, causing the captain's hand to jerk and his knife to gash my left cheek from temple to chin. I close my eyes, allowing the lack of gravity to swallow me whole. My fingers explore the left side of my face, feeling the raised line of skin.

I've been bottling all this hurt for decades; I can feel the seams ripping, and I'll eventually rupture, pouring out all my innards, my pain, my everything. But at least then, it'll all be over. That incessant question bites my brain stem yet again: Will life get better?

"Dan, Dan, Daniel! Man, you good, bro? The logs were still hot, and you plunged your hand in the firepit. Look at your hand; it's bubbling," Quo says, kneeling over me, wide-eyed and slack-jawed.

There's a serpent in my stomach, writhing in all the acid and beer. The worst hangover. "Turn off the halogen. It's piercing my eyes. Motherfucker. What did you give me?" I say, with one eye open and my left hand clenching my seething abdomen. I sit up and try to make a fist with my right, but the nasty sting shoots to my elbow. The center of my palm is reddened, blisters forming in a familiar… geometric pattern.

What the fuck?

"Gotchu," Quo says, switching off the lamp. "Bro, I gave you a taste of a drug I've taken many times. Shit, I never threw my hand into a bonfire, though. What'd you see? Where'd you go?"

"How long was I out?"

"Forty-five seconds, maybe a minute," Quo says, eyeing me like a freak. There's no way that was only a minute.

"I need to sleep," I say with finality, shifting onto my knees, aged bones cracking and popping until I'm standing. Without the lamp, I can see only Sequoyah's silhouette, and he's nodding without a word. "Osda usvi." I've picked up some Tsalagi from Quo over the years, but I know very little.

"Osda usvi, tsosdadahnvtli."

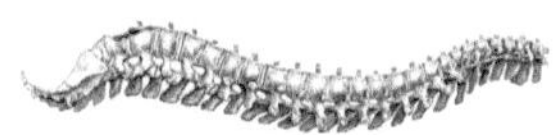

I lie supine in bed, spinning red ambulance lights bleed through the blinds and cast shifting shadows across my walls. My television doesn't get watched as much as my ceiling does, always squinting, trying to derive meaning or some-such significance laced in the popcorn spackle's random pattern. A beer-soaked sigh exudes from my gullet, filling the room with despondency. Can't sleep. Haven't really since I cut my camping trip short with Quo a few days ago. Those visuals. Those memories. I'm feeling grimy, like a jelly made of those ants is caked all over my body.

As soon as my feet hit the floor, I'm pacing straight for the bathroom and taking off the rest of my clothes. There's a fire lit under my ass to twist the shower knobs and wash myself of everything, scrub it all away.

I hop in, ignoring the usual ice-cold spray before the water heater gives a shit. Shampoo first, then body wash. With my double-sided back brush, I'm furiously scrubbing at my chest, arms, and hands. The coarse bristles rip away the filth, taking hair follicles and peeling back my epidermis with it.

"Look beneath your skin," a little girl's voice says.

The back brush hits my toe, and I hold the shower walls for stability. The voice was clear as day, though distant. My eyes dart around the bathroom and out the door after I yank open the curtain. Nothing. Twisting the knobs to stop the water, I crouch to wield my brush just in case. My ears are straining to hear something—anything—out of the ordinary. My ceiling fan is clinking, a car is coasting by, and my dehumidifier is whirring on low. I wait a moment longer before exiting the shower, drying off, and growling into my towel to muffle my anxiety.

Slipping my boxers on, I tell my Control Unit to raise the lights and turn off the fan. The voice calls out again, but it's garbled as though whispering from the apartment corridor.

I approach my front door, an aluminum bat behind my back. I'm cognizant of the fact this might be a hallucination, but Quo reassured me the trip doesn't return like an earthquake's aftershocks. Setting my eye against the peephole, I'm unable to detect anyone or anything through the minute fisheye lens.

The voice echoes again from behind me, though it sounds like it's gurgling blood and the person is sharing their last words. The voice's notes are sustaining and drawn out. I flip the bat up to grip it from its center and advance toward the noise. As I draw nearer through the dining room, the gurgling seems to reverberate from my armoire. My ear presses against its ornate wooden door, but the voice stops. I sidestep the armoire and crouch to observe my dehumidifier; it's about three-feet tall, white, and has an indicator light for the drain tank. The voice is burbling louder than ever and, once I touch the dehumidifier, the LED goes from white to red, signaling the tank is full of water. Squinting as if that will protect me, I pull the tank's handle to slide it out from the unit.

A bloated, pallid child's head is in the tank's water.

The aluminum bat clangs to the tiled floor as I stumble backward, my cavernous mouth unable to produce a sound. It's the little girl who died at the lake my foster family visited one summer. I couldn't save her because I didn't know how to swim, and my arms weren't strong enough to undo whatever held her legs in the murky depths. The last thing I saw from the lake dock was her ashen face blinking, accepting I couldn't save her; I sealed her fate. Her face has haunted me for years.

"*Lobobok benbeabth yobur skiibin,*" the head coughs out, water spraying my dining room floor. My tumultuous heartbeat stands me up, and my foot smashes the tank back into the white apparatus, sloshing more water onto the tile. All my brain's synapses are Tesla coils, firing and sparking, shooting my blood pressure sky high and my anxiety even farther. Without thinking, I sprint to the bathroom, slam the door shut, and lock it.

My breathing is coarse, the thickened air from the shower filling my lungs.

"I'm in control. I'm in control."

While pacing what little space I have in the bathroom, I repeat my therapist's mantra ad nauseam. Centering my thoughts is proving difficult, so I cower to the slick floor in a fetal position and concentrate on my breathing. The phrase from the elderly woman and the little girl at the lake echoes through my mind endlessly. With my head near my knees, I gaze down my legs at the half-healed scabs that stretch toward my shinbones. Beneath my skin?

The knotted scab on my right knee peels far easier than I expect, but it snaps away early, leaving most of the scab intact. I turn the broken piece over in my hand, and I swear I'm seeing a pattern that couldn't be there, like my ceiling. White etchings line the back of the partial scab, along with incredibly faint lettering.

Gulping, I stand and exit the bathroom. My neighbors can probably hear me stomping toward my kitchen, but I no longer give a fuck about a low profile. I pull open a drawer like a pinball plunger, with enough force to jumble the organized utensils.

Serrated knife.

My swiping arm sends all the kitchen table's contents to the floor, and I place the broken scab etching-side up, raising my leg on a chair to saw off the rest. For once in my life, I'm lucky for being so meticulous and always sharpening my knives. The scab separates from my bleeding leg like butter, the knife slicing to the shin. The long strip resembles a bloody piece of gyro meat. Its backside has more white lines, some crossing, so I lay it on the table. Warm blood trickles off my leg and onto the wooden chair. Switching legs, I repeat my slicing motion, but cut too deep near the shin, sending fiery ice up my body. A grimace masks my face as I grit my teeth, nearly cracking my crown. With a little more finesse, the second scab strip severs and joins the other.

What adorns my kitchen table reminds me of the jigsaw puzzles from childhood—the only toy they ever gave me. I could never finish them before Paul entered my room and undid the pieces, shouting at me to tend to the crops.

Using the knife's point, I pop the blisters on my right palm. The puss oozes down my wrist, and I think to grab a dish rag to bite for what's coming. The serrated blade allows me to saw back and forth across my hand, and the smell reminds me of the slaughterhouse once we got pigs in. Blood is pooling on the floor in a maroon lake, and the pain forces me to sit for the rest of the sawing. If not for the rag, my teeth would shatter.

My unique palm print smacks the table like a piece of black forest ham.

"Control Unit: Call Sequoyah, burner phone seven," I say, hunched over, wrapping my exposed hand with the food-stained dish rag.

"Aye, homie. How you been?" Quo says, happier than usual.

"Sup," I say, holding the pain back behind my teeth, "Are you able to stop by?"

"Okay, okay. What are we fixin' to do? How's your hand?"

"That's why I'm calling. Have any pain meds? Something that will murder the pain but not put me into a coma."

"I think I got whatchu need, man. Be there in like forty?"

"Sounds good. And Quo, bring the DMT."

There's nothing but a static hum between Quo and I for a moment, then he says, "Be there in forty."

"Jesus fucking Christ!" Quo screams after I unlock and open my front door. "What the..." His eyes are doing all the talking.

"I know, I know," I say like a tired schoolteacher.

"The fuck happened to your skin? You're all red, man."

"I'll tell you as soon as I get these fucking pain pills, hermano."

Quo zips open his fanny pack and rips through its contents before handing me a generic orange pill bottle. "Take two, pronto. Shit, maybe even three."

After reading the label, I bark, "Ibuprofen? Are you fucking kidding, bro?"

"¡Chupa mi verga! The label don't match what I got in the bottle, fucker. Shit's fentanyl, but not that whack shit with bath salts cut in." Quo gets heated whenever I question him, but he quickly returns to baseline after looking at my flayed body again.

Three is too hard to swallow with spit, so I wash them down with the rest of an old beer can near my sink. "Look at the table. You got the DMT, yeah? Spirit Molecule and all?"

For the first time, Quo gets a glimpse of the table covered in hundreds of gobbets of my skin, and his eyes once again become satellite dishes, transmitting the ultimate, "What the fuck?" signal possible.

I thrust my chin at the table, saying, "Look closer. What do you see?"

Inching toward the skin puzzle, Quo traces his hand along the table's edge, as if he's afraid of his knees buckling. "I see Turtle Island. Fuck is this? You skinned yourself and drew a map of Old America?"

"The drawing was already beneath my skin. Didn't draw shit. That vision quest you sent me on, or whatever the fuck you want to call it, out by the creek? The visuals brought me some place with entities or memories, or I don't know what the fuck. And they all repeated the same line: 'Look beneath your skin.' My whole life I've wondered where I'm from. This is supposedly the answer."

My raw, moist index finger points to the skin map. The white etchings form the United States, with all those imaginary state borders they created back then, complete with labels for every Indigenous nation's homeland—at one point or another because some are nomadic. There's a black shape that traces around a section of the map, what they used to call the Midwest, including Settler States like Montana, Wyoming, North and South Dakota, Colorado, and others. In the center of that shape, black text reads: Tsistsistas.

I turn to face Sequoyah, tears gliding down my cheeks, and say, "I'm Cheyenne."

My body is weak but free of pain. Quo helps me to my bed to lie down again.

"Here, cover your eyes with this. It helps," he says. Quo hands me a plush baby blanket, which I assume is to obtain some level of sensory deprivation. His hand is boring into his fanny pack again, pulling out a pipe, a sack of milky-white crystals, and a torch lighter.

"Aight, so we're gonna freebase it out this pipe. Check it. Got this tiny mesh screen at the bottom of the pipe to catch the extra—don't wanna waste. I'mma put the crystals in, hold the flame underneath the bowl, and you're gonna take at least three giant-ass hits, hombre. Got it? Then you lay back and go where you go."

"Why's it look like crack? Damn, better be the right stuff." I sit up, straining the visible muscle in my gut, and notice my sheets are red as hell. Quo holds the pipe up for me, and I bring it to my mouth. The torch's gas is audible and the flame waves back and forth underneath the pipe. As the crystals melt, Quo nods for me to inhale. Years of cigarettes have prepared me for this long drag. I take it in slowly, feeling the smoke fill my mouth. After I don't think I can suck in more, I waggle my eyebrows at Quo and pull it all into my lungs and hold my breath as long as I can before choking. A cloud of spirit molecule rushes out of my mouth, no cough. Quo helps me repeat this twice before lying down and covering my eyes, but before I can blow out the third toke, I'm free falling through the bed and across the universe.

At first, it's just darkness, the back of my eyelids. Then my eyelids pulse, and I wonder if the vague shapes and colors I'm seeing are from my overtaxed mind. A brilliant splash of blue and purple hit the background, and geometric patterns line the walls as though a Diné weaver has decorated this space. The pattern matches the elderly woman's handkerchief. As I focus on her, she reappears before me but without the black void eyes or the insects. This time she has no sunglasses, and her amber eyes are kind.

"Are you Navajo?" I ask.

"Are you Cheyenne?" she asks.

"You showed me I was."

"I did nothing. I'm glad your friend brought you back to me."

"Why's that? And why were you so frightening last time?"

"Don't recall any fright."

"The bugs, the swarm?"

"How many times did you breathe in the magic crystals?"

"Just three times. Are you a spirit?"

"Three is good. Means you have a direct connection to this world."

"What world is that? Where is this place? Is it another planet?"

The elderly woman doesn't respond. Her eyes point my way, but she isn't seeing me. Her body has a subtle sway to it, like she's in a trance.

After I blink, she's lunging at me, her gaping maw wider than humanly possible. But she doesn't physically hit me. Her essence flows into me like a ghost, sending me spiraling through space. Instead of twinkling stars, syllabaries of an old language I don't know paint the atmosphere. The twirling is like the world's worst come up, vomit locked and loaded for spurting across time and space.

My fleshless hand pats my face, and I can tangibly feel it. I rip off the baby blanket, and my world reverts to my bedroom, Quo standing by my side. I'm dizzy, and my lungs explode. A pale cloud surges from my mouth and forces its way into Quo's mouth and nose. He backpedals as if hit by an uppercut and nearly tumbles to the ground.

Fire eats my brain, and my stomach is ready to projectile all over the walls. My eyes meet Quo's, but his face is shifting. His jawline juts out then sideways, temples and forehead bubbling, melting down like molten metal. Quo's body lurches and shifts, his shoulders and back arching into a geriatric posture plagued by arthritis.

The elderly woman stands before me.

Fuck, fuck, fuck! My brain can't figure out what to do, so I spring at the evil spirit with my left shoulder and knock her to the floor. Cutting right, I slide across my tile floor to exit my bedroom and grab my baseball bat on the living room sofa. As I turn around, it's lunging at me again, its sharp claws scratching at my ribcage, tearing raw muscle off in chunks. Gripping both ends of the bat, I'm shoving it against her throat, blocking her snapping jaw lined with long, razor-edged teeth. Her claws are going too deep, and even the opiate's fading now. With all my might, I shove her into my wooden armoire, giving me enough room to take a stance with the bat.

The spirit eyes the serrated knife on the kitchen table and looks back at me. It sprints at the table, arm extended to grasp the blade. My swing is out of reach, and I miss completely, but I cock my arms back again. The thing is acting playful, tossing the knife back and forth between both hands while we circle each other in the living room. It thrusts at my face, the notched blade slicing down my cheek. It's too close, so I take a few steps back to get a good swing in, and I trip backward over my fucking ottoman. With angry glee, the ugly fucker pounces toward me, and I position the bat to strike it in the abdomen, knocking the wind out of it. Adrenalized daddy longlegs dance up my spine and down my limbs, pushing me to stand and face my fears. I bring the bat up and behind my back to bring it down onto the elderly woman's cranium, smashing her skull with a satisfying crack. It falls to the floor, a sea of black oozing out of the head and across the tile.

The thing's body cracks and pops, shifting into something else again.

It's the little girl from the lake.

Her cold, distended corpse lies before me, water leaking from her orifices and mixing with the blood from carving myself. Her head turns toward me, and after coughing out a lungful of moss and lake water, she says, "Deeper. Look deeper beneath your skin to know who you are. Where you came from." Her sorrowful eyes just stare into my soul before she's no longer animated and her head thuds to the floor. The being is shifting once more, and I'm crab walking backward to put some distance between us.

Sequoyah lies on his side, brain matter and blood draining from his skull.

THE GREAT MOMENTUM OF DOUBT

by John F.D. Taff

He wasn't given the choice, but had he, the thing he'd want to remember about Beth as they descended that final incline down the mountain was her face. So happy, so filled with life and love, like a filament of sunshine right there in the passenger seat.

"Darling," she'd said in an affected, Audrey Hepburn voice. "I was made for a day like this."

The sun had been the problem, the single reason Mike would cling to in the weeks following, the endless *whys* and *what ifs*.

In the most meaningful of ways, his life after this was simply a continuation, tumbling over and over, just as the car had.

As if it had never come to rest.

The blinding glare of the setting sun—its dramatic and unrealistic foreshadowing—had caused him to turn from Beth, so exuberant, shoes kicked off, laughing at something he'd just said. No hint of the fight they'd had that morning, the acrimony, the words finely honed to soul-piercing tips. No hint of the turning of her ring around her finger, as if measuring the circumference of its significance. What it might mean to lose it, toss it aside.

No, just pure joy. Of the day spent together, of the vibrancy of their relationship when left to its own devices, free of the anxieties or neuroses of either of the pair.

Then that ruinous sun, flashing into view as they crested the top of a particularly steep rise, set-off with one of those cartoonish signs of a truck nosediving down a wedge.

He'd been laughing with Beth, drawing in whatever he could to hold in reserve for the increasingly common bad times, something warm and happy to sustain him through the thrown hairbrush or car keys, the cat-spit of angry words, the one-handed clap of slammed doors.

What he was left with was that brief, heartrendingly sweet picture of her, laughing, happy.

He laughed, too, checked his rearview mirror, the road ahead.

The sun flash that blinded him.

The car ahead, which he swerved to avoid.

The metal shrieking of the guardrail as the car parted it like scissors cutting the ribbon of an opening ceremony.

As it dawned on him things had gone astray, he reached across the console, took her small, warm hand, sticky from the carnival food she's stuffed herself with that afternoon.

Seconds before the car struck, nose down, flipped over and over, landing belly up and canted jauntily against a boulder, he turned, tried to burn her happy face into his brain, perhaps the last thing he'd see, the one image he'd take to guide him through whatever afterlife would follow.

What he got instead was a view of a paper cone of red and blue spun cotton candy held between them, its ball of fluff blocking her face, so much so it seemed the cotton candy *was* her face, her hair billowing around it in the death physics of the tumbling car.

The rolling light of the murderous sun, still descending in the west, uncaring of what it had done to them, revealed Beth with a cotton candy face, a distended, carnival-colored thing.

He didn't realize until much later in the hospital Beth *hadn't* been eating cotton candy in the car late that afternoon on the trip back to their little Nashville apartment.

That tidbit of reality didn't matter, though.

This was his last memory of Beth, red and blue face swirling in the tumbling, sudden stillness of the wreckage.

Even stiller, in a casket.

Mike had insisted on attending her funeral. *She was my wife*, he told her parents. But he had *broken a femur*, three words that were not enough words to describe what the accident had done to Mike.

It had shattered the bone of his left leg, necessitating screwing the severed halves of his knee joint back together and hammering a steel rod up the unbroken length of bone to join with the reassembled joint. It made the compound fracture of both arms seem piddly by comparison.

He insisted on being at Beth's closed-casket visitation, at her funeral, at her burial, so his father had pushed a comically complicated wheelchair down the aisle of the church, the broken leg propped straight out, both arms in casts, held in place by a rigid rod between them. Couldn't walk, couldn't even wheel himself to be there for

Beth as she was laid to rest in the crowded urban cemetery where her parents had already bought a plot for her.

No plot, he thought sourly, for him.

There were lots of firm handshakes, gentle pats on the back, sticky kisses from aunts and aunts-in-law, distant cousins. A meal slurped in the church basement because their apartment wasn't large enough—and he was still technically in the hospital anyway. His parents had fled to that Southern asylum known as Florida many years ago, so they couldn't host at their house.

Beth's parents, as prickly as she could sometimes be, didn't even offer.

So, school kitchen chicken and dumplings and ravioli to celebrate the love (supposed) of his life.

Mike fed by his mom, felt the heat rise in him, the indignity of it, for him, for her, the incongruity of it, spoon fed like a baby after burying his wife.

When his parents wheeled him back to the hospital, they left him seething with the fire ignited at the funeral. Those flames engulfed him, carried him off to sleep where the only thing he saw, the only thing he remembered was hair crashing like waves into Beth's red and blue swirled face, rotating in the car. Laughing. Laughing.

Laughing.

"Darling…"

The weeks of his healing went by both agonizingly slow and blurringly fast. Mike received few visitors during the three weeks in the hospital, mostly just his parents. Beth's came once, right before the funeral, but never after. He knew, with no real closeness and no grandchild to cement them, he'd most likely never see them again.

Which was okay, since they reminded him of Beth, of mostly the bad parts of Beth. In her mother's tight, grimacing smiles and her father's offhandedly hurtful remarks.

Honestly, he wouldn't miss them.

Mike spent his days in therapy of one kind or another, walking the halls of the hospital or using the parallel bars in the physical therapy gym. The therapists urged him to get up and walk more, to strengthen his leg muscles, to get his digestive system back in order from the pain medications he was on.

He spent his evenings grieving his dead wife, dreaming of her almost every night. For a while, they were happy dreams. How they'd met, the dates they'd been on. Cooking in their tiny apartment kitchen. Snuggling on the couch for Netflix nights.

After a week in the hospital, though, the dreams changed. Maybe his boredom seeped into them. Or the sourness left in Beth's wake. Or the self-pity he was barely able to keep in check.

I'm a widower, and I'm only twenty-seven!

Whatever it was, it crept in slowly, tinging his happy dreams in small ways. Cooking together ended in a weird dish of crawling worms and bugs with oversize mandibles worryingly sharp. Date night ended in a gunfight at the theatre, Beth and Mike munching popcorn obliviously, watching the carnage around them as if it were part of the show.

Netflix night ended in an argument that took them off the couch, tumbling down a steep incline, shouting at each other as they fell. Along with the grasping tree limbs whipping him, he felt car keys and hairbrushes orbiting as they fought.

Sure, that particular nightmare scenario—at least the fighting—had happened in real life enough times.

The night before Mike left the hospital, though, his dreams went back to the accident.

Tumbling in the car.

Beth's face, though, steady, not circling like everything else in the rotating interior. Focused on him.

But *not* Beth's face.

A puff of cotton candy, swirling red and blue, seeming to frown at him, piercing and malevolent.

In that dream the night before he left the hospital, he reached out to her, his arm penetrating the debris circling inside the car to touch her cheek tenderly.

His fingers came back sugar-tacky, red and blue.

Mostly red, though.

Mostly red.

His parents helped him to an apartment now seeming like one of those tombs they hack out of the sand in Egypt. Frozen in time, set with furniture and tchotchkes mired in liminality, stuck between states of being.

As he stomped in with his walker, meticulously outfitted with tennis balls by his father, he noticed dust lay thick over everything, though he'd been gone less than a month. A slight quip about this, meaninglessly uttered in low breath, sent his mother attacking the dust as his father stood by nervously watching him maneuver to the couch.

After a few moments of shooting the shit, his dad launched himself up, went to the car to get the rest of his stuff. He'd never been one to sit and talk, and having all this down time at the hospital sitting and talking had worn on the old man. Before they'd left, he'd gladly taken the walker and personalized it with tennis balls from, as he noted several times, his own tennis bag. It was something he could do for his son, something Mike knew he was *willing* to do for his son.

When his parents left, he was alone as he'd ever been in his life. This loneliness was a new construct, a tent erected on a single pole—the loss of his wife. She'd never return from wherever it is she'd gone.

She hadn't left him alone for a night out with her friends. Or to grocery shop. Or spend some time with her mother.

Beth was gone.

Permanently gone.

This singular fact would be driven home in the weeks ahead—alone in the endless hours of insomnia laying in bed dissecting the minutiae of their relationship, alone in the endless hours of the day sitting on the sofa dissecting the minutiae of their relationship.

There was nothing too slight, too meaningless to spend hours splitting apart. The weird look she'd given him over a hamburger on their last evening out before the carnival. The constant worrying of her wedding ring on her finger, a nervous habit (but was it?) he'd noticed only a week or so ago. How she checked on the mail two, three, four times a day on Saturdays when they were both home, as if expecting...what? Coupons in the local circular? A check from Publisher's Clearing House?

Any of these, *all of these*, played on his mind in an endless reel, interrupted by meals, sometimes by a show he found on television to divert his attention.

The one thing, though, that ate at him more, was why he dreamt of Beth with that cotton candy face. It wasn't just in the car, right before the accident when the late afternoon played on the honey chestnut of her hair. Nor was it only during the accident, when his entire world spun, except for the sugary billows of her red/blue face.

No, now it was all the time, in every dream, every memory, even the absurd scenarios his dreaming mind concocted for whatever occulted reason it did these things. A dream of being late for the airport, trapped at the front desk as he tried to settle his bill. Across the counter, Beth, dressed in the prim blue outfit of a hotel employee, pert little tag with her name engraved.

Her face the ridiculous cloud of cotton candy, subtly swirling as he watched, red and blue and red and blue.

Or his memory of sitting outside a café in Paris during their honeymoon. The little chairs were hard and uncomfortable, so she'd slipped off her shoes, curled her bare legs under her. Her knees exposed by the beautiful sundress with its repeated pattern of dragonflies flitting over it.

They'd eaten, drank a bottle of wine, tiny cups of espresso.

And laughed.

"Darling," she'd said, pinky up as she lifted her cup.

He couldn't see her smile anymore, couldn't see the pout of her lips, the freckles over the bridge of her nose, the slight gold tinge to the iris of her blue left eye.

Gone. Only the impassive wisps of cotton candy.

Mike mentioned this to his mother on the phone after returning from one of his numerous PT appointments. She'd pressed him repeatedly about why he sounded down, not at all like himself. As if he should suddenly, miraculously be cured, of his broken limbs, of his dead wife. Just be over it because it was so inconvenient to others.

Surely the doctors have prescribed a medicine, the physical therapists have worked a muscle that would put this all behind you by now.

In a pique of anger, Mike told her one of his dreams.

When he reached the point of Beth's face being replaced with cotton candy, his mother gasped and dropped the phone.

There was some fumbling, then his father's voice.

"Don't burden your mother with your nightmares!"

His father hung up, leaving him staring at the receiver. Had his dad ever hung up on him before? He didn't think so.

Why was that aspect of his dreams, his memories, that single aspect bothering him so much? He couldn't think why. Couldn't think why the mere mention of it would bother his parents so much.

The hospital case worker recommended a grief counselor to help him navigate through these dark waters, as she'd put it. He'd nixed the idea almost immediately in the initial shock of his grief.

Now, swaddled in the spin of his thoughts, navigation assistance seemed like a good idea.

The counselor's office was in one of the low buildings spreading out from the main hospital complex. This one was filled mostly with psychiatrists and cardiologists, which made Mike laugh.

Heart and mind.

He signed in, waited in a small antechamber with one rickety table covered in a stack of thin, semi-recent magazines like *People* and *Us* and *Entertainment Weekly*. After a few minutes, the counselor ushered him into her office. It was all done up like an Ikea ad. Very minimal with cool, blonde furniture both spare and uncomfortable. Utilitarian.

Renata was her name, and she sat opposite one of the uncomfortable chairs, waited for him to take a seat. She wore a thin sweater, buttoned at the top, a pair of glasses on a beaded chain, like a somber librarian.

"So, Mike, how are you?"

He wasn't reticent at all, as he thought he might be. He simply gushed it all out, how he felt, how he perceived the world to be in the new light of his overwhelming grief.

Even his dreams and nightmares.

He wiped his eyes a lot with the box of tissues on another rickety table near his chair. She took copious notes, scribbling in a small black journal, looking up to skewer him with her dark, piercing eyes.

They spoke of Beth's face, the cotton candy.

Renata stopped writing, clicked her pen.

"Mike," she said. "Do you think this might be the way you're processing the fact Beth was decapitated in the accident? That they haven't yet recovered her head? Perhaps it's a sign of any guilt you might feel about what happened?"

The sudden drought in Mike's mouth glued his tongue to his teeth.

"What?" was about all he could manage.

She what?

They haven't what?

What? The? Fuck?

He waited two days after his counselor's bombshell to call his parents. His father picked up the phone. He knew before any word was spoken, by the fumbling of the phone, the hoarse clearing of a throat.

"Hello?"

"Dad, it's me."

"Hey," he said, sounding wary, as if he were really saying *Look, we're not going to talk about your goddamn dreams, are we?*

Instead, "How are you?"

"The counselor let something slip in my session a few days ago, and I wanted to hear the truth from you."

Another uncomfortable throat clearing, and Mike knew.

"Well, what's that?" his father asked, as if he were guarding an entire nest of secrets.

"About Beth. About her losing her head." He couldn't bring himself to use the word *decapitation.*

"Shit, Mike," his father breathed heavily into the phone, lowering his voice, Mike guessed, so his mother wouldn't hear. "We were trying to protect you, understand? There was so much going on, what with Beth's passing, the arrangements, all your injuries. Did you know they were going to remove your spleen and gall bladder? For some reason, didn't at the last minute. The compound fractures, the—"

"Dad," Mike said. "So, Beth did lose her head?"

"Yeah," his dad said, sounding defeated, as if the loss of her head was due to some failure on his part.

"The counselor said they hadn't found…it."

"Fucking counselor," his father muttered. "That mountain is pretty steep there, as you…know. The cops weren't sure exactly when the loss occurred. So, it could be just about anywhere. Thrown from the car, bouncing down the mountain, carried off by an ani—"

"Dad! Jesus, just…just slow down. Ease off, okay? I guess I should have been more coherent, should have asked about the closed casket."

"Look, you were injured, pretty damn seriously, and we were worried about you. It just didn't seem the time or place to tell you. Afterward, no time or place seemed right."

"No need to apologize," Mike said, putting a hand across his forehead. "Just another thing to process, really. Got a lot to put into perspective these days. What's one more thing really?"

"Wanna talk to your mother?" Universal dad-speak for *This call is now over*.

"No. Thanks for being honest with me."

"Always."

Mike hung up.

The counselor had been right about Beth's cotton candy face being a manifestation of his guilt. He had been driving after all. He'd been the one who thought he saw a car, swerved to avoid it, sent them careening down a mountainside.

Just one niggling detail.

He'd begun having this dream, this memory, weeks before he learned of her decapitation.

Where was this coming from?

On the phone with the captain in charge of the accident investigation, wanting to know more about what had happened, in the accident, to Beth.

"I'm calling about Beth. I had no idea my wife's…ummm… was…ummm."

"*Decapitated*." Mike was sure the cop felt he was throwing him a lifeline there, but he wasn't. Not really. "Yes, unfortunately she was."

"Her head hasn't been found?"

"No, sir. Not yet. We've scoured the area twice with teams, but so far nothing."

"But you haven't finished yet. You're not giving up."

"Sir, as you know, the terrain there is pretty steep. Craggy. Doesn't lend itself well to searches of any kind. We can't risk the lives of our cadaver dogs there."

"Fuck the dogs. This is my wife's *head*, for chrissake!"

"I know, and I'm sorry. What I was trying to impress on you was how difficult the search was."

"*Was*? As if done and over, right? *Sorry, we haven't found your wife's head. Go fuck yourself.*"

"Mr. Hendrick, sir—"

"Well, what have you been doing since you're evidently not looking for my wife's head. What about the car I nearly hit?"

"You said in our interview you'd swerved to avoid a car ahead of you," the cop said, in stereotypical detached cop-speak. "Is that still your statement?"

"Well, yeah. I mean, is it supposed to change?"

"No, sir," the captain said. "Just checking to see if you might remember anything else. We've got two eyewitnesses coming eastbound up that same mountainside who back up your recollection."

"So, that wasn't just me hallucinating from being blinded by the sun?"

"No, sir. We'd like to talk to the driver, charge them with reckless driving. Maybe even manslaughter. We're looking for a red Buick Riveria, probably early nineties model."

Why did that car description set off the trombone sound he used to hear in television game shows when someone lost?

Mhwaaaaaawwww.

Mike's grip on the phone slipped, and it thunked on the carpet, the battery cover popping off.

When they'd first met, Beth drove a 1992 red Buick Riviera.

If the police couldn't find her, then he had to.

At least that's what he thought when he awakened late morning, sun highlighting the weirdly thick motes swirling in the air of his room, glinting like a scatter of fairy dust.

He prepared for the day, took a careful shower, sat on his bed to put on his clothes. His arms were still sore, weak, even though the casts had been removed. Socks were now the enemy, as he had problems bending, lifting the broken leg off the floor to slide a sock on.

In those minutes, he talked himself out of free climbing down the side of some mountain searching for his wife's missing head. How could he, given his broken leg, his healing arms? He couldn't drive yet, even though the casts had been removed. Everywhere he'd gone over the last few weeks had been by Uber. Imagine trying to explain *that* trip to an Uber driver.

Instead, he fixated on the car the cop had described, the red Buick.

Beth's car.

That was flatly impossible though.

They'd traded in that particular car early in their marriage, to buy her a sleek little Volkswagen. Surely that car, by now thirty years old, was in a junk yard, stripped of its saleable components, squashed into a cube of metal, melted down.

Mike told himself this all through breakfast. Repeated it as he tapped the Uber icon on his phone, entered the address he wanted to be taken to that morning.

Beth's old apartment.

It was just as Mike remembered it, the apartment complex on the east side of town, out toward Lebanon. Same grey paint with blue trim. Bland, but kept up.

The cars were all the same, though. Sure, they were newer models, but still the same bland sedans and trucks in bland colors—black and whites and navies and greys. Same number of years on them, same bland owners. Dental hygienists, retail store managers, nurses, office workers.

Mike had the driver creep through the late morning parking lots surrounding the complex's six main buildings. Many cars were gone, off to work with their owners.

As they got closer to Beth's old apartment, Mike experienced two overwhelming thoughts.

What the fuck am I doing, casing my wife's—my dead *wife's—old apartment?*

What if the car was *there?*

The car because it couldn't possibly be *her* car.

He asked the Uber driver to slow.

There, squatting toadlike in the sun-scatter, was the red Riviera, rusting along the back wheel wells, tires worn, paint flecked with mud, as big as a boat.

Beth's car.

His dead wife's car.

Sunlight sparkled from the strip of chrome wrapping its rear bumper, polished, almost mirror-like, excited phosphenes in Mike's eyes.

Coincidence. Had to be. Some other woman had the car now. Some other woman had the car and lived in Beth's apartment complex.

He asked the driver to wait, but the guy begged off, said he had other fares. Maybe he'd be available when Mike was finished. He offered to help him out with the walker, but Mike demurred.

Once out, the driver sped away. Mike was left standing in the parking lot of his dead wife's apartment complex. Brought back so many memories. The first night he'd stayed over, waking in the morning at her place and going to work grinning like an idiot.

Sneaking up on her when she'd gotten off work another time, surprising her with a bouquet of roses and an invitation to dinner.

Arguing with her standing by this very same car, bitter words, the jingle of keys hurled at his head, missing him and tinkling away into the bushes.

Fights on the little balcony where they'd cook out sometimes. Fights in the stairwell getting the mail.

Fights, fights, fights. They were what crowded forward now, what dominated his memories.

Why those? Why not the sunny, smiling Beth, light playing on her hair, her hand in his, small and warm?

He walked away, then stopped, walked back to the car. Peering in the window, he could see her winter coat, not hanging in the closet but wadded up in the back. So Beth. Receipts littered the floor, mostly from the fast food she ate at lunch. Dry cleaning tickets.

As he was bent over, staring into the car, he heard a noise. The soft clearing of a throat.

He turned to see her.

"Excuse me, dude, why are you so interested in my…Jesus fucking Christ!"

It was a girl, but not Beth. She had blonde hair verging toward strawberry. Petite, thin, pale skin.

She was holding something before her, a bottle of mace or her keys gripped like Wolverine's claws, he wasn't sure. He didn't focus on that.

He put up his hands to show he wasn't a threat to her, but it had the opposite effect, even with the walker. The girl stepped back, fumbled her phone out of her purse.

"Stay back, you fucker. I'm calling the cops."

"My face," he croaked. "Do you recognize me? Is that it?"

"I have no idea who the fuck you are."

"Then what is it about my face?"

"Look!"

He bent to the side mirror of her car.

Expecting to see his familiar visage—the square cut of his jaw, the whiskers from not shaving that morning, his bleary, exhausted eyes.

What he saw instead drove him back, back from the car, back into the parking lot, then clomping away ridiculously with his walker, down this street and that, acting from the muscle memory of a decade ago.

He found himself winded at the front of the complex, crossed the busy street to a shopping center, caught his breath there.

The face he'd seen in the mirror was a puff of cotton candy, swirling blue and red, blue and red.

He never saw a cop go into the apartment complex. Evidently the woman had chalked it up to some random, harmless weirdo, gone about her business. A different Uber drive brought him home. This one watched him nervously in her mirror, and he wondered if she saw it, too, the cotton candy face.

Of course she didn't. She saw a man wigged out of his mind,

breathing a little too quickly, sweating. That's what she saw, not a cotton candy face.

She said nothing, dropped him off at their apartment—*his* apartment now—and left quickly, just in case.

He fumbled his way inside, pushed the walker across the room and flopped on the couch. The overworked muscles of his left thigh—the ones the broken bones of his femur had sliced through—twitched in protest. His arms throbbed from all the work they'd done keeping him standing, leaning onto the walker.

He considered gulping a painkiller or at least a few aspirin, but before he could act on it, sleep slipped in and quieted the chorus of pain.

He awoke, thought he was still in the tree limbs at the accident site, hanging above some unseen bottom far, far below.

He'd dreamt he was back in the car, sailing off the shoulder of the road, through the guard rails, tumbling, tumbling.

Beth with her eerie spiraling cotton candy face.

They were plunging through the tree limbs, snapping branches as thick as his thigh. Or was that his *actual* thigh shattering?

He was sweating when he came to, his arms slung out.

He clambered up, staggered to the bathroom. What time was it? What day was it? He knocked two aspirin into his hand, added a pain killer from the prescription bottle whose contents were dwindling.

Who cares if he ran out? There were always plenty more to be had, even in mid-opioid-crisis America.

Hesitating for only a second, he swallowed a second little pill.

When he began to feel their effects, he used the app on his phone to summon a car.

The driver was not happy about stopping on the side of a highway and letting him out. Mike, though, was persistent, almost pleading.

Mike watched him drive slowly away, merge into traffic, shaking his head.

The guardrail here had been recently repaired, a new section in place where the car parted it. He ran his hand along the length, warm in the afternoon sun, gritty with the dust of eighteen-wheelers and family vans and luxury sedans flying past it every day.

Over the railing, and he stood on the edge of a great drop, a steep hill descending and descending, through the tops of countless trees. The highway had been blasted through the midsection of a good-size chunk of foothills, slopes to the greater mountain chain, and the terrain along the road was treacherous, steep and craggy, with trees clinging to its rise and fall with the tenacity of mountain goats.

Mike stared into this, steeled himself. His broken leg was stiff and sore, difficult to move. His arms, free of their casts, were still not fully functional.

Still, he placed a foot on the lip of the drop, stepped down. Immediately his footing was unsure. A trickle of rocks and debris rained down the hillside as he found purchase. He reached out best he could to catch a tree limb, hoping to steady himself.

It didn't do what he'd hoped, and he stumbled forward, his foot catching the edge of a buried rock, tripping him, sending him lurching downward. Tree branches whipped at him, and he used his arms to slow his fall.

A solid limb caught his stomach, and he folded around it, stared down through the tangle of trees. A bumper, ripped from either the front end of their car or the back. A piece of a headlight. A spangle of broken glass.

Grunting, he unpeeled from the branch, lowered himself farther.

All kinds of detritus now, rusted pieces of metal, clutches of wiring.

Below all this, almost lost in the shadowed undulations of earth and forest, a dark, hulking shape canted against the steep drop of the hillside.

The car. *Their* car. Still here, resting where it had fallen.

Scrambling, he swung and fell, scraping the heels of his hands, smudged with dirt and marked by swipes of tree sap.

The car, felled like a buffalo on the great plains, belly up, lay there on a little outcropping of rock. Mike breathed heavily. His leg was on fire. He looked up, saw he'd come down nearly a hundred feet or more.

He grunted in appreciation of his accomplishment, sweat dripping from every pore, not just from the exertion but from the pain his earlier medications were barely keeping at bay now.

But there was the car, the thing he thought would hold all of his answers.

What answers? some dim part of his brain asked. *To what questions?*

He ignored that particular inner turmoil, dropped to the upturned bottom of the car, scrambled for purchase over it, careful not to fall. He saw it had landed on the last possible outcropping before another two or three hundred feet to the scrub floor below.

It seemed damp here, smelled of mildew and the rot of wood and small plants, leaves and fir needles. He could also smell rusted metal, burning rubber, the tang of gasoline from the wreck.

He stepped across its underbelly, found footing enough to squat near the passenger side window, its shattered glass rendering it open.

Slumped inside, hanging upside down from the still clasped seatbelt, was a body.

A spray of hair, seemingly brown in the shadows of the car's interior, covered its face.

Did they leave her down here? Was that it? They didn't just give up on finding her head, they left her entirely down here to rot with the wreckage of the car they obviously found too inconsequential to bother trying to haul back up to the road.

That couldn't be. He had buried *something*.

He was dreaming this, hallucinating.

He reached out, to touch the ghost or corpse or whatever this was, to rouse her, and the thing spun its head as if it were on a spindle, revealing familiar red and blue wisps of cotton candy.

The stuff parted, a dark hole resembling a mouth, and screamed, so loud and so high-pitched he flinched, nearly lost his balance.

From out of the car came something, a metallic glissando immediately remembered.

Thrown keys.

They struck him square in the center of his chest, like a punch thrown by a prize fighter.

That was what pushed him over. His fingertips, mostly useless, scrabbled at the windowsill, found no purchase there. Backwards, his arms pinwheeling, his shoes kicking vainly at the black loam.

He fell, crashing gracelessly from limb to limb, like a pinball moving from bumper to paddle. Down, down, rebreaking one arm, then the next. A branch catching his forehead and ripping off a flap of his scalp, blood flowing freely. Another twig punctured an eye.

Broken, bleeding, he finally dropped to rest, his breath gone, pain flaring. He licked his lips, tried to see with his one remaining eye.

Turning to accommodate what felt like broken ribs, he coughed a wad of blood, tissue. Had he bitten off a chunk of his tongue? Yes.

But there, oh there, laying beside him was Beth.

At least her head.

It was turned away, but he moved one broken arm, nudged it over.

The head was as battered as his, more so. In addition to the injuries it had sustained from the accident, animals had gotten to it, gnawed her lips and most of her eyelids away. One eye dangled from its socket. Her hair, always so luxurious and golden-brown, was dark, matted with blood and pine needles and ants.

All Mike saw, though, was her cotton-candy face, swirling red and blue, blue and red.

She rolled closer to him, pillowy lips puckered.

Cotton candy swirls, and he kissed her, kissed her, kissed her…

"Darling," she said.

"The closer to the truth the lie is, the more likely they'll buy it. Understand?" Eddie, to his younger brother, summer 1985.

8TH MAY 2022. 2100HRS P.S.T.

TRAVIS TANNER: "You're listening to the Crime Time podcast with myself, Travis Tanner, and my good friend and retired police detective, Bob Erskine. We've been talking to our guest, a man often known simply as 'Carly's dad,' David Scott. David, thanks for being with us tonight. We're going to go to the phones soon. But first, let's return to your new book for a moment."

DAVID SCOTT: "Yes, *Carly's Wish*."

TT: "And you're about to head off across country on a book tour to promote it…"

DS: "Yes, starting next week."

TT: "Now this comes as we approach something of a grim milestone in Carly's case. In a little over a week, it'll be ten years since she disappeared, at just six years old, from the Fort George State Park."

DS: "That's right. On the 15th."

TT: "And, if you don't mind me asking, what will you be doing on the 15th? It's a dark day, do you have any plans to mark that day?"
DS: "I'm doing a reading and a signing in Vegas that night. I'll be doing what I've been doing every day since Carly was taken, talking about the case and my search for her."

TT: "I can't imagine, as a parent, how I would feel in your shoes. I feel like I might crawl into a hole, just shut down, disappear from everything, but… somehow you've, for want of a better word, you've, er, thrived, been driven by this. I mean, this is your second book, the first was a best seller, adapted for a movie starring Tom Selleck, the case was featured on *Unsolved Mysteries*. I've heard that HBO is planning a series adaptation later this year. What does *Carly's Wish*, the follow-up to *Carly's Dream*, bring to all this?

DS: Well, I guess people will have to read my book to find out.

TT: Er, I suppose that's true.

Bob Erskine: So, David, we've talked before. This isn't the first time you've been on our show, and we've discussed most of the theories of the case. The main three, I'd say. Does the new book detail any new theories? I'm sure our listeners would love to hear if any new information has come to light.

DS: *Carly's Wish* documents the past five years, my search for Carly in the time since *Carly's Dream* was published and the case first got any real media attention. I mean outside of here in Maine, that is. I suppose before *Carly's Dream*, I was screaming into a void. Now people listen to what I have to say.

TT: Okay, we're going to go to the phones now, but before we do, can I ask what *Carly's Wish*, your new novel's title, refers to?

DS: To Carly wanting to come home. That's her wish, obviously, to come home.

TT: Well, the switchboard is buzzing, let's go to our first caller…

TEXT SENT FROM DAVID SCOTT'S PHONE.

SUNDAY, 8TH MAY. 11:08 PM.

DAVID SCOTT:

Usual waste of time. True Crime kooks and rubberneckers mainly, a few kind old dears, and some fuckwit reading tea leaves. Fucking tea leaves.

GIL CRAWFORD (DAVID'S AGENT):

What? Who even makes tea with leaves nowadays?

DAVID SCOTT:

Kooks. Did you hear from Kaplan?

GIL CRAWFORD:

They'll cover your stay in Vegas, if you set aside the afternoon of the 14th to talk to the documentary crew.

DAVID SCOTT:

Good. Speak in the morning.

Walt squinted at the number on the cell. He held it closer to the pickup's cabin light and checked it against the email printout. He didn't want to admit it, but he was getting to the age where he needed a phone with an old-man-sized screen, as his daughter liked to tease him.

"Fifty-two is not old," he told her, but right now his eyes begged to differ. He dialed the number. As he waited for it to be answered, he watched a moth bounce along the windshield, trying to get to the light inside.

"Hello?" The voice answering was rough, woken by the call.

"Hello? Is this Mr. Scott? David Scott?"

"What? Yes. Who is this? Do you know what time it is?"

"I am so sorry. I'm travelling interstate" Walt lied. "Isn't it eight a.m. where you are?"

"Uh, no, it's just after four in the morning? Who is this?"

"I heard you on the Crime Time podcast." Walt watched the moth beat against the windshield, fall away, and fly into it again. It wasn't taking *no* for an answer.

At the other end of the line, David sighed. "Okay, look, I don't know how you got my number…"

"Your agent gave it to me. Mr. Crawford."

"Alright, listen, if you've got a tip, call the police, please. If you read some coffee grounds or something like that, call a priest."

"Ten years ago, I watched a man drag a six-year-old girl out of the woods at the Fort George State Park and into his car. I thought she was likely his daughter, but it was odd enough that I followed them."

Walt didn't wait for David to reply. He ended the call. He wound down his window and took a deep drag of the cold morning air. *You don't get fresher than Maine air,* he thought. Not that he'd ever really left the state in his fifty-two years. He threw the phone out onto the verge. It landed face up, the screen blinking on when David called back. Walt flicked off the cabin light and started the pickup. As he drove away, he wondered if the moth would be drawn to the glow from David's call.

Don Gilbert took the cell phone out of the display cabinet behind the counter. He locked it again but didn't bother to take the key from the lock. Small-town security. He placed the box down on the countertop and then turned it over again to find the barcode.

"You starting some kind of criminal enterprise?" he asked Walt. "This is the second one of these cell phones you've bought from me in the past two weeks."

"Don, if I'd taken to a life of crime, don't you think I'd drive a better pickup?"

"Well, you got me there. I was watching a documentary on the, you know, er, *Discovery Crime,* or something. This hitman, when they catch him, he's got four, or was it five, different cell phones. Never made more than one or two calls on 'em before he threw them out. No one could trace him."

"'Cept the police who caught him, I guess."

"Haha, yep, that's true."

"I took the last one fishing with me. Next time you're out on Jackson Lake, if you're lucky you might just reel it in. Fell out of my pocket, over the side the boat, and that was that. And my Kelly wants me to get one of those expensive contract phones, you know, with the big screen. What am I going to do with one of those? Buy some of those Kryptonite Coin things?"

"I hear ya. You say hello to Kelly and to Meg for me, will ya?"

"Will do, Don."

Monday, 9th May. 11:12 AM.

Gil Crawford:

> Not since that private detective. And I wouldn't again. Not without talking to you first. Why?

David Scott:

> Got an odd call at 4am this morning. They said you gave them my number.

Gil Crawford:

> Not me. 4am? What did they want?

> Tea leaves?

> Lol.

David Scott:

> It was just weird. I'll call you when I get to the signing.

David slipped his cell into his jacket pocket and disappeared back inside his house.

Walt had parked his pickup across the street from David's gated house. He'd watched him ferrying luggage from the house into the trunk of his silver Lexus. From the open trunk lid, he knew he'd be returning with more packing soon. Walt wondered how much David's place was worth. A million dollars? More? How much did a bestseller and a TV movie go for these days?

David appeared again, weighted down with a large overnight bag, trying to keep hold of a box filled to the brim with books. Walt hit the green call button on the disposable cell and waited.

David half dropped, half spilled the box of *Carly's Wish hardbacks* into the Lexus's trunk. The overnight bag followed them in. Walt watched David fumble the phone from his jacket, and then he hung up.

Walt waited another ten minutes, until the driveway gate opened and David was driving down towards the street, before he called again. The Lexus stopped where Walt could see David clearly.

"Do you want to know what I saw that day?" Walt asked.

"Of course I do."

"It'll cost you $5,000. Bring it to Fort George State Park tomorrow."

Walt could hear the disgust in David's voice.

"You think you're the first person to ask for money to tell me what happened to my daughter? How many times in the past ten years do you think I've heard the same *clues* recycled from true crime forums? The dreams of amateur psychics? My own fucking book read back to me? How many times do you think someone's put a price tag on the truth about my daughter—"

"I don't know what happened to your daughter."

"What?"

"I just know where she went. Where she was taken. You want to know, you'll bring the money and be waiting for me at five a.m."

"I could just call the police right now…"

"And tell them what? That you don't care what happened to your daughter? After ten fucking years, I'd be begging to know. Five a.m. tomorrow. $5,000." Walt hung up.

He left David sitting in his driveway. If he was being honest, he had a hard time looking at David. He had a lot more to say, but that would have to wait until they were face to face. On the way home, Walt stopped at Jackson Lake. He walked to the end of one of the jetties and threw the cell into the water. He imagined Don Gilbert hooking it next time he was fishing out there, pulling it, bewildered, into his boat. On a normal day, that might have made him smile, but right now he felt that there was very little to smile about.

Meeting at five a.m. meant by the time they got moving the sun would be rising, and David would see everything Walt wanted to show him. It meant they'd almost certainly be the only ones in the parking lot. It also meant that David would be unlikely to see Walt watching him from the tree line when he drove into the lot. If, of course, he came.

David pulled in at 4:56.

Walt kept him waiting until ten after five before stepping from the trees and onto the gravel parking lot. Ten years is a long time to keep a secret. Another quarter of an hour wasn't going to change the truth.

Walt knocked on the Lexus' rear windshield as he approached. The sound of knuckles on glass set David spinning around. For a moment, Walt thought he was going to bolt. Instead, he watched Walt's wiry figure shuffle along the side of his car and come to a stop by his door.

After a time, David wound down his window. Walt guessed he'd been taking that time to rehearse what he was going to say.

"Well, I'm here." David gestured to an envelope on the passenger seat next to him. "That's your money. You want it, you tell me what you saw that day."

"No."

"What?"

"I'm going to show you. Hand over your phone."

"Why?"

"Because I'm pretty sure you're recording this, and I don't want to star in your next book. Hand it over."

"I'm not going anywhere with you."

"Okay." Walt turned and began to walk away.

"No, wait…I—"

Walt stopped, "Look, mister, you can sit there and hem and haw about this, but I start work in just over an hour and a half, and so if we don't get going soon, we really ain't going anywhere."

"A…Alright, okay." David reached into his jacket pocket and took out his iPhone. He handed it to Walt. Sure enough, a sound graph scrolling across the screen, with a timer running above it, indicated that David's phone was recording.

"I, er…" David fumbled to explain himself.

"I don't care. Of course you were going to record me. But you'll just have to remember what I said for your next book, okay? Now"—Walt handed the phone back—"turn off the recorder."

"What?"

"I don't know how your damn phone works. Just turn it off. And delete the recording."

David took the phone back. He hesitated, wondering if he switched out of the app it'd keep running in the background.

It was too risky. He decided to do as he'd been told. He stopped the recording, deleted what he'd captured, and closed the app.

"Alright. Leave your phone in your car."

Walt waited. He'd expected David to argue, but instead he sat looking up at him. Maybe he was weighing his options. After a time, David opened his glovebox and slipped his iPhone inside.

"Follow me." Walt could sense David's reluctance as he climbed out of his car. Good, he thought. "And bring the envelope."

The sky above them had begun to lighten. As they crossed the parking lot, a whippoorwill lamented the arrival of dawn, calling close by in the woods.

"You ever seen one?" Walt asked.

"What?"

"A whippoorwill. Often heard, but seldom seen, isn't that what they say? If you hear one, then something bad is gonna happen to you. Of course that's bullshit, otherwise bad things would have happened to most everyone I know."

"I don't believe in that sort of superstitious rubbish."

"Yeah you do. Remember, in your first book, *Carly's Dream*. You said that a day or so before she disappeared, she told you she had a dream she was in a dark place and couldn't get out. It was maybe a cellar or a trunk, you wrote. Not sure why you called that a dream. Sounds like a nightmare to me."

"Like the entire past ten years then, huh?" David lit a smoke, drew deeply on it. Walt had left the parking lot and wandered onto a track heading into the woods.

"That scene in the movie, when that girl actress was trapped in the trunk and she could hear the guy approaching. Holy cow, I barely slept for a week after that. It didn't happen though, did it?"

"It was a movie, they take liberties with the truth."

"Not the *movie*. The dream in your book. You made that up, didn't you?"

David took another deep drag. He looked off into the woods. "Where are we going?"

"Did you even write that book yourself? I heard when you get a deal with a big New York publisher, they set you up with one of those ghostwriters who does the work for you, you just put your name on it."

"Are we going somewhere or just talking?"

"Haha! I knew it! I wish someone would go to work for me." Walt left the track and began to trudge through the brush. "Careful here, it's treacherous," he called back to David.

On the track, the first grey light of the morning had begun to bleed through the canopy above. As they left the dirt path and headed into the woods, thick branches twined above, holding in the night for a while longer yet.

"Where are we going?" David asked again.

"We're taking a shortcut."

"It doesn't feel like it." David ducked under a low branch. His ankle rolled as he put his foot down on the uneven ground and he almost lost his balance. "Shit!"

Walt called from ahead, "Here we are."

They'd arrived at a smaller parking lot. A wooden post-and-rail fence bordered three sides, a dirt track led away on the fourth. Walt clambered over the fence and crossed the lot to his pickup.

"Ten years ago, I was parked up here, along with a couple of other cars. I saw a man drag a young girl out of the woods"—he pointed— "coming from that direction. There wasn't a fence there then."

"I didn't even know this lot was here."

"It's not for the public. It's meant for the rangers. This used to be where people came if, you know, they didn't want to be disturbed."

"What were you doing here then?"

"Get in the pickup."

David joined Walt in the truck.

"Back then, I was a recovering alcoholic. By recovering, I mean I was out here drinking. Guy strides right past the front of my truck. Maybe he hadn't noticed I was sat here, maybe he didn't care. He pretty much throws the girl into his car." He pointed again. "It was parked there. He guns his engine and gets the hell out of here."

David took out another smoke.

"Don't light that in here."

Sheepishly, David put the cigarette away. "What happened next?"

"Well, I was pretty out of it, wasn't entirely sure what I'd seen, thought maybe it was a father and his little girl, you know how kids throw tantrums. They can scream blue murder. But, no, something felt off. So, I followed them."

Walt started up the pickup and pulled out of the lot.

They drove the dirt track in silence, the pickup rocking and jolting over the uneven road. Walt drove the track like he knew it, too fast for David, who clung on to the grab handle above him. Eventually they arrived at a wooden gate, propped open, and beyond that, to David's relief, the rough road turned to asphalt, and they left the woods behind.

"I heard you on that Crime Time podcast—"

"You told me that. Where are you taking me?" They'd left the track, but David still held on to the handle.

"You've done a lot of talking over the past ten years. A whole lot of talking."

"What's your point?"

"How much *looking* have you actually done yourself?"

"It's not that simple."

"Like that day in the park. What were you looking for then?"

"What?"

"I heard it was tail. That you'd arranged to meet up with a woman there."

"They printed that in the *Herald* just after my first book came out. That's not new information."

"Still, you took your six-year-old to a park so you could hook up with some pussy."

"That's not how it was. I don't have to explain myself to you."

"You do if you want me to tell you what I know." Walt slowed the pickup. He peered out of his driver's side window into the tree line. A break in the trees revealed an overgrown track.

"Nah, I don't think that's it."

Walt continued on.

"Do you actually know where we're going?"

"It's been ten years, okay? Things have changed. So, what were you doing in the woods that day? *Hiking?* That's what you told the police at first, isn't it?"

"Look, it wasn't just some random hookup, okay? We'd been talking online for months."

"Well, that makes all the difference."

"Okay, look, my marriage was failing. My wife, she drank. She drank a lot. She was an alcoholic. It was..."

"Wait..." Walt looked off to the right. "This looks promising." He swung the pickup off the highway in a way that made David glad he was still holding the grab handle.

They'd turned onto a partially graveled road. "Yeah, this is it. I followed the car along here. Your wife's dead now, though, right? Drank herself into the ground, huh?"

"Why are you showing me this now?" David scanned their surroundings, "Why didn't you come forward when Carly first disappeared?"

"I didn't need the money then. I need it now."

"That's it?" David spun around. "You knew what happened to my daughter, and you didn't come forward because you couldn't make a buck out of it?" He grabbed at Walt's shirt.

"Look, I already told you, I don't know what happened. I just know where she went. Now, you can either sit back, shut the fuck up, and I'll take you there. Or if you want a fight, I'll kick your ass and leave you by the side of the road. Which is it to be?"

"I...I'm armed, you know." David had already dropped his hand away, though. He leaned back in his seat.

"Why? Are you afraid the truth's gonna hurt you?"

Ahead, the road twisted a sharp left. Walt followed it around, and in the clearing before them was the house.

The old clapboard house had likely been white once. Now its boards were the color of bones, shrunk and split from years of neglect. Mold had spread across them like decay between stained, old teeth.

Walt pulled up and killed the engine. "This is it. This is where I followed them to."

David looked from Walt to the house. The porch had partially collapsed. Its sagging eave reminded David of a drooping eyelid.

"They went inside there." Walt wound down his window. The cool morning air made his skin prickle. "I had other stuff I had to do and so I left."

"You did *what?* Why would you do that? Wasn't it obvious that something was wrong?"

"I told you. I had other things I needed to get done."

"You're lying! You just drove me out here for the money, didn't you? Admit it! You heard me on the podcast and thought you could make a quick buck."

"No. But I don't much care if you believe me or not. That's what happened, and that's your five grand of information. Now pay up and get out. I can't sit here talking to you all day."

"No, you're lying. You have to be! If you'd seen what you said, you'd have reported it, surely. You'd have told someone before now, when there's nothing that can be done." David grabbed at the passenger door handle and threw the door open.

"Look, I told you what I saw. I told you what happened. I might've sat here for another ten, maybe fifteen minutes after they went in. Didn't see anything else, didn't hear anything."

"I have to go inside"

David was already half out the door. Walt sighed. "Yeah, I thought you might say that."

"And I'm taking your money. You want it, you'll come with me."

Walt hung back, watching David stumble through the knee-high grass as he headed for the house. He hadn't lied about what happened ten years before. He *had* sat in his pickup outside this house. He'd even parked pretty much where his truck was now. He sighed, kicked at the dirt caught in the pickup's treads, and then began to trudge through the long grass after David.

The house's windows were shuttered. They'd been closed the last time Walt had been there, too. *See no evil*, he thought.

David leaned close to the flaking slats, trying to look between the boards and see inside. He forced his fingers under one of the shutters and pulled at it. A stream of dark sludge slithered off the sill, drooling over David's hand and down the front of the house. Likely rain, blown in and trapped by the warped shutters; its dark appearance and stench made David think of something putrefying.

"Christ!" he snatched his hand away, wiping it on his pants.

"Maybe we should try the door," suggested Walt.

A tattered fly screen was latched shut over the front door. Its gauze had long since parted company with the frame. It likely hadn't stopped a fly in years. Walt pulled the screen open. David tried the door. It swung back into a hallway the color of nicotine.

A stained towel had been thrown onto the bare boards of the entrance hall. Like the outside of the house, mold had begun to spread over it.

David leaned into the hallway. He stopped, listening, feeling incredibly vulnerable. At any moment, someone could rush at him from one of the doorways off the corridor.

The house remained silent.

David stepped inside. Walt followed.

They moved through the house without speaking. Each room they passed seemed to be more chaotic than the last. In one, possibly a living room, vinyl flooring had been pulled up and rolled back to reveal the filthy boards beneath. Against the wall, newspapers had been stacked from floor to ceiling. A dark bloom of mold spread from the stacked papers across the yellowed tiles above. *Everything is rotten here,* thought David.

Walt stepped around a pile of empty food cans that had been built into a pyramid in the middle of the hallway.

Where there wasn't detritus, there was dust. The air was thick with it. Walt held his shirt cuff over his mouth and nose. The way David moved in fits and starts, Walt could tell he was close to turning tail and running.

When he'd unlocked the house that morning, before heading to meet David at the park, he'd considered that David might not have the nerve to go inside, that he might take more leading, more motivation than Walt's story provided. If he turned to bolt before they arrived at the locked door ahead, Walt's plan would have to change.

They passed a kitchen, a bedroom where a mattress had been propped up against a single bedframe like a kid's makeshift fort. Underneath, more mold-covered newspaper, and a bowl a dog might've eaten from. A rope had been tied to one of the legs of the bed, its other end lay frayed beneath the 'fort'.

"Dear God…" David choked out the words.

The tub in the bathroom was filled with more half-eaten food cans, jagged metal edges glimmering where they'd been pried open, and their contents spilled and smeared over the plastic.

Ahead, David stopped in his tracks. A door off the corridor had been fitted with a large padlock. The heads of the screws holding the hasp in place stood out from the metal plate, allowing David to open the door a crack before they stopped his progress. He rattled the door against its lock.

"I think I can open this. Can you give me a hand?" David leaned against the door.

Walt had loosened the screws himself. They were about to find out if he'd loosened them enough.

The two men shoved against the door. The first time, the hasp held. They shoved again, and with the sound of splintering wood, the door was thrown open. It slammed back into the bare brick wall behind it, revealing a set of wooden stairs falling away into the darkness ahead.

David rocked forward on the top step. Walt grabbed the back of his jacket and held him.

"Thanks." David put a hand on the doorframe to steady himself. Walt continued to hold onto his jacket.

"Is it really concern for you daughter that brought you here?" Walt's grip tightened.

"What?"

"I mean, if she's dead, if she died ten years ago, she doesn't give a fuck about your search, does she? She can't."

"What are you saying?"

David tried to shake Walt's hand off his back. Walt held firm.

"Or is it guilt driving you? That you left your daughter with another kid younger than her, with your date's little boy, while you took your friend for a *walk* in the woods."

"Fuck you. You don't know me." David pulled against Walt's grip.

Walt looked past David, down into the darkness ahead of them. They could both smell the metallic stench rising from the cellar.

Walt waited for David to buck against his grip one last time before he let him go. The father tottered on the top step.

"Maybe you're right," Walt continued. "I guess I've only really heard about *you* until now. You want me to leave? I'll take my money and go, if you like."

David didn't answer. He swept a nervous hand over the cold brick wall, feeling for a light switch. He found it and flicked it.

Nothing.

He took a hesitant step forward. Walt followed him down.

With each step, the stench grew stronger. Behind David, Walt retched. They'd soon left behind what little muted light the house offered.

They leaned against the cold cellar wall, fingers slipping over the damp bricks, feet cautiously finding the wooden steps, testing the warped wood before putting their weight down upon them.

David stepped onto the soil floor of the cellar. He felt the earth slip and give under his weight. His shoe sank into the wet ground. Behind him, there was a click as Walt switched on the flashlight he'd been carrying in his shirt pocket.

"Seriously, you had that on you the whole—" David's words died as he saw where Walt's flashlight beam had stopped. "Oh, dear God."

In the corner of the cellar, slumped against the wall, was a corpse.

David raced over to the body, although it was more of a pile of bones wrapped in rags. He skidded, almost falling onto the remains. Even wasted to almost nothing, it was clear that the body had once been an adult. The bones were too large to be a child's. David grabbed at the clothes, pulling them away from the wall, scattering the bones across the floor. Maybe he expected to find something beneath the body, maybe it was just panic driving him. He spun away from the wall, frantically searching the cellar floor around him. Walt tried to follow David, light his way with the flashlight. That didn't stop David from tripping over the shattered remains of an ornamental owl statue. He lost his footing and slammed down into the mud.

Walt helped David back to the stairs and sat him down.

"She's not down here. It's just him."

"How? How do you know that?"

"Well, I lied to you."

"What?"

"I lied to you to get you here. And I lied when we were in the truck just now."

"I…I don't understand."

"I did follow him and Carly from the park. I followed them the way we drove, out to this house. I watched them, like I told you, watched him drag her inside. I sat in my truck, smoked a cigarette, and… I almost left. But I didn't. I followed them into this house."

Walt wandered over to the owl statue. He pulled its considerable weight from the mud. One of the owl's wings had been smashed off.

"Coming up the corridor, I could hear them down here. I could hear her fighting him, trying to fight him off. He's making this weird, whining sound, halfway between a child and some kind of an animal. Then there's this thud. Stopped me dead. You know, the kind of sound that just screams something's wrong. After that she wasn't fighting him anymore."

Carrying the statue, Walt crossed back to David.

"Well, I picked up the first thing that came to hand. This fucking owl statue. Weighs a damn ton. I almost dropped it down the stairs. I'm not sure how I did it, but I managed to get pretty close to him before he realized I was there. He's got his pants round his ankles, down on his hands and knees in front of where she's laying. And he's making that noise, only it's getting louder, louder and he's getting ready to… Christ, to do whatever goddam awful thing he was planning to do to her. And, for a moment, I thought *he's an animal*, he's an animal somehow dressed in a man's skin. How could he not have been seen for what he was when he was in that park? How did he manage to walk among the rest of the people there and not be spotted, not be seen for what he was?"

Walt held the statue with white knuckles. "I took this statue, and I brought it down on his head. I brought it down again and again. He scuttled into that corner, whimpering and holding his hands up, trying to protect himself. Well, that just made me angrier. I hit him so hard that I snapped the damn wing off this thing. I remember hearing the bone in his arm crack, it bent awkwardly, like an arm shouldn't, and just fell useless to his side. I smashed his skull until I was covered in his animal blood. Until he was barely recognizable as either a man or a beast."

David's voice was a hoarse croak. "What? What happened…"

"Carly was on the floor, over there." Walt pointed with the remaining wing of the statue, "He'd cracked her head pretty bad. I scooped her up, carried her out of here, put her in my pickup, and I drove away."

"What?" David tried to stand up, but Walt pushed him back onto the stair. "What happened? Was she dead? What did you do with her? Tell me! You have to tell me!"

"No. No, I don't. While all this was happening, what were you doing? Chasing pussy? I don't think you'd even realized she was gone by the time I was picking her up off of this floor."

"What? Please… What did you do to her? Why didn't you bring her back?"

"Yeah, I thought about it. I watched you giving a press conference that evening. The one at the park, with all the cops gathered around you. Remember? You were talking when you should have been out there looking. Talking, like you've done for the past ten years."

"What did you do to her?"

"She told me about those nights when you left her, left her with a mother who could barely look after herself, let alone a six-year-old. What were you doing those nights?"

"Please. What did you do with her?"

"She said you'd roll in late, if you came home at all, drunk and whispering on your phone, arranging your next date. She used to lay awake listening."

"Are you telling me she's alive? You bastard! What have you done with her?"

"I didn't do anything with her. I let her decide what she wanted to do. That's what I've done for the past ten years. And that's why we're here today."

"What do you mean? You've got to tell me where she is!"

"No. I'm not going to do that. I'm here because she asked me to give you a message."

"What?" David was on his feet now. "What message?"

"You should have been a better father." Walt struck David with the owl statue. The blow knocked David back onto the stairs. He threw up his hands to try and deflect the blows, but they were useless against Walt's strikes. Walt brought the statue down again and again until there was no doubt that David was dead.

Walt had bought several padlocks from Don Gilbert's store over the past few months. He fitted a fresh one to the outside of the cellar door. He fitted another on the front door of the house. He hoped he'd never have to set foot in that foul place again. After that, he drove to a motel, where he rented a room for cash and showered for the best part of an hour.

Kelly was sitting on the porch bench when Walt pulled the pick-up into the driveway of their small house. She'd chosen the name Kelly herself. It was close enough to Carly that she'd thought it'd be easy to get used to.

Walt joined her on the bench. "Here." He passed her the envelope with David's five thousand dollars in it.

"I don't want this."

"I know. But I'm gonna hold on to it for you, case you change your mind."

"It's done then?"

"Yeah."

"Thank you. I couldn't stand to listen to him anymore."

"I know."

"Ten years of whining how he loved me so much. Podcasts, television, that awful movie, like he was the fucking victim in all this. If he'd loved me so much, he wouldn't have lost me in the first place."

THE ELEVEN FILMS OF OONA CASHFORD

by Gwendolyn Kiste

The Oona Cashford Film Festival
Pittsburgh, Pennsylvania
October 2022

The indelible Oona Cashford is unfortunately not a name widely celebrated in the cinematic canon. Hers is not a name known to almost anyone these days. Arguably the most overlooked female filmmaker in horror, her work has slid into relative obscurity, resurfacing only in the midnight movie circuit. This retrospective will allow us to examine her impact on the genre as well as explore what happened to her and—perhaps just as importantly—what happened to her most devoted fans, many of whom have been reported missing over the past two decades.

This commemorative booklet will feature commentary on all of Cashford's extant films, as well as excerpts from interviews with her associates, including her long-time collaborator and muse Grace Oliver.

The purchase of this booklet will also admit you to our weeklong film festival. However, please be warned in advance if you or anyone else attending a film screening inexplicably disappear, we assume no liability for the incident. We're only showing the films, not attesting to their effects on others.

Thank you in advance for your support of our cinematic preservation efforts, and as you enjoy the film festival, feel free to tag us on social media using the hashtag #OonaCashfordLives.

Untitled #1

Oona Cashford's first foray into film can be described as modest but promising. With a running time of only nine minutes and three seconds, it's a straightforward enough story. A young woman wearing a thin veil wanders around a blooming garden, the colors as bright and blazing as the spring. There are flowers in her hair, and her feet are bare and dirty. It seems as though the film might venture into traditional fairy tale territory until the sky goes suddenly dark, and the young woman finds herself besieged by an army of tiny, razor-clawed creatures. Her arms flailing, she makes a valiant attempt to flee, but ultimately, the ravenous creatures consume her, flesh and bone, her end a most glorious sight to behold, the blood dripping Technicolor red down the screen. The film cuts to black with no credits.

Despite the attempts of many enthusiastic fans, nobody has ever located the actress in the short. Some say if you look close enough, it's Oona Cashford herself, grinning out at the audience from behind the veil. For the purposes of this retrospective, we won't comment on our own theory, and instead, we shall allow viewers to decide for themselves.

The film was not without its own set of problems. There were rumors festivals had a difficult time showing it, due to an infestation of rats seeming to follow wherever the film went. But for what it's worth, we could confirm none of these reports.

All that really mattered was the short caught the eye of a small movie studio, which offered to fund Oona's next picture. If only they'd realized what they were about to unleash.

Menagerie of Death

Oona's debut feature never racked up many blockbuster receipts, but it did rack up its own kind of notoriety. The story was certainly a schlocky daydream. A down-on-their-luck family inherits a haunted zoo and must band together to fend off a vicious menagerie of ghost animals. Throughout its ninety-minute running time, there are no less than a dozen maulings from tigers and lions and even one particularly surly otter, each attack shown in brutal, loving detail. (Nobody was ever sure how Cashford could so realistically depict a jugular being torn from a throat, the blood spraying toward the camera like a gruesome fountain.)

In the end, the family manages to gather the animals together and create a fearsome fortress of hungry phantoms, training the beasts to consume anybody who attempts to pester them.

"Nice wholesome fun," Oona beamed at the time. Then just for good measure, she promised that no animals were harmed in the making of the film.

"Only ordinary people," she said, and flashed that killer smile of hers that could charm anyone in a hundred-mile radius.

Big Top Chop Shop

With her notoriety already established among a small but growing set of fans, Cashford's second feature was an equally gory outing about an ill-fated couple on a trip to a carnival run by cannibals. It also featured its own promotional tie-in: barf bags handed out for free at the concession stands. And as silly as it seemed, at least a couple patrons in the audience were always grateful for them. After all, this feature had even more torn flesh than the last, and in spite of herself, Oona Cashford's antics soon had everyone talking.

"A female William Castle," a few reviewers called her.

"The New Queen of Schlock," according to others.

"She certainly loved a good gimmick," said her longtime muse and lead actress Grace Oliver.

Big Top Chop Shop marked the first collaboration between Oona and Grace. They met shortly after *Menagerie of Death* had its premiere, and the two were soon inseparable, never leaving each other's side during filming, never wanting to leave each other at all.

"Oona was a genius," Grace said in an interview with us last year. "She could make you believe almost anything."

We asked about exactly what she wanted Grace to believe, but we never got an answer. Instead, Grace only shook her head.

"Like I said," she murmured, "she was genius. She understood things the rest of us couldn't even begin to imagine."

If the Door Bolts Behind You, You Know I'll Be Waiting

Cashford's next film is a gothic potboiler of sorts, with all the typical trappings of a Brontë knockoff. A brooding estate, a brooding hero. Darkened shadows and darker secrets. A corseted damsel in distress—played of course by Grace, who blushes and blooms in every frame, looking perfectly incandescent no matter what kind of light fancies her face. There was talk that her on-screen glow was due to her off-screen antics. A gossip column even caught a few candid shots of Grace and Oona during their free time away from set, their hands wrapped together, besotted smiles on their faces.

"I have no interest in discussing our personal lives," Grace said when we asked, and she threatened to walk out of the interview if we inquired again. But by all accounts, she and Oona enjoyed a brief period where even the paparazzi couldn't break their stride, the two of them hidden away in hotel rooms, room service trays piling up at the door, their crystalline laughter echoing through long hallways, sounding like freedom.

There's another rumor that's dogged this film from its earliest release. According to cinema legend, one devoted fan brought a Super 8 camera into a late-night screening outside of Cleveland, excited to catch the looks of gleeful terror on the audience's faces. And he caught something all right, even though there's debate to this day about what it is.

It happened during a scene halfway through the film. Grace's character is racing through a dungeon, desperate to outpace her past and a bevy of creeping insects keeping pace with her as she flees. Only once she escapes, slamming the stone door behind her, the bugs decide they're not done yet. They decided they've got someone else to terrorize—namely, the audience themselves.

All at once, the bugs pour through the screen, breaching the fourth wall like it's made of air.

Everyone who was there swears it was all for fun. "Just a silly promotion," they said.

But for anyone watching the grainy Super 8 footage, it doesn't look like much fun at all. Instead, if you zoom in for a closer look—and of course, we've zoomed in—you can see there are cockroaches everywhere in the theater, twining up pant legs, diving into soft drinks. They're on the walls, the rafters, the railing. They're seeping through the screen like spots of motor oil. And in a corner seat in the front row, you see one particular bug that doesn't simply skitter over a woman. It skitters *into* her.

"More gimmicks," Grace said when we asked her about the video. "And don't get me wrong. The gimmicks were great. But Oona had more to say than just barf bags and plastic bugs."

Except when you watch the video, you can't possibly believe those bugs were anything but the real deal.

"They were *plastic*," Grace insisted. "I promise you. I saw them."

But that's not what we see. It's a cockroach, as alive as you or me, and once it disappears into the female fan in the front row, it never emerges again, its carapace lodged somewhere within her, merging with her. Becoming part of her.

(Side note: we've tried to locate the nameless fan from the video to get her side of the story, but unfortunately, she wasn't available. Based on what we can deduce from the local papers at the time, she disappeared shortly after the screening. Or perhaps, she even disappeared *during* the screening.)

It's also worth noting that something changed with Oona Cashford after this incident in Cleveland. Cult classic historians claim she soon began her descent into what some call a special sort of genius, and others refer to as a special sort of madness.

"It was her ultimate obsession," Grace said. "To uncover the secret of film itself."

Oona began talking at length about a theory of hers, something she'd been developing for years, trying to coax out with film techniques. Something about a strange membrane, what she called the boundary that separated us from the world of cinema.

"Oona thought she could breach the barrier," Grace told us. "She thought if you tried hard enough, anyone could breach it. That we could waltz into a movie like it was only another room."

And fans are still debating whether or not that's precisely what she did.

Slash by Numbers

Even with the growing lore around her films, Oona Cashford could barely gain any traction in the media. It was as if her work would appear, make a regional splash, and dissipate again just as quickly.

Grace exhaled a harsh laugh when we asked why she thought this happened. "Because," she said, "men are allowed to be visionaries. Women are barely allowed in the door."

But nobody could say Oona Cashford didn't have vision. She had enough vision to inspire fans to try things we still can't fathom, not even now.

The plot of *Slash by Numbers* was—what else?—a standard slasher with some of Cashford's extreme panache thrown in for good measure. Slit throats, slit wrists, enough gore to soak right through the screen.

And that's exactly what happened, at least in one theater in Des Moines. At the climax of the film, Grace's babysitter character is fleeing the killer, as a bucket of blood is poured right at the screen. But instead of hitting the camera and stopping there, the blood did something else. It came right on through, leaking down the walls of theater and onto the floor, coating the plush seats, coating every pair of sneakers.

There were screams for a moment and then no screams at all, as more and more blood poured out of the movie, drowning the audience, drowning everything. Broken bodies floated toward exits, so many of them there was no way in or out, their figures piling up against doors, their limp limbs bent backwards.

At least until the movie was over. Because when the lights flickered on, so did everybody else. The patrons staggered to their feet, shaking their weary heads, before starting out into the lobby, seemingly none the worse for wear.

"The usherettes were literally cowering in the projection booth while the movie was playing," the theater owner told us, "but afterwards, everything was fine. It was just a prank, I guess."

"Is that what they think?" Grace asked us when we told her this. She considered for a moment. "It's probably best they keep on believing that."

Sister Skin Savior

This should have been enough to establish Oona Cashford in the horror canon. But despite all the chatter about the films and their infamous screenings, most people still don't seem to remember her. It's an odd anomaly, as if the world itself is doing its very best to delete her.

"It's so easy for the world to dismiss a woman like her," Grace said. "Someone so strange. So uncompromising."

Of course, it didn't help that Cashford's most ardent fans have dropped off the map, one by one, as the years have gone by. It became a sick kind of dare, one that was almost a rite of passage. First, you've got to attend a midnight screening of one of Oona's films. Any of them would do, though *Sister Skin Savior* is a particular favorite.

"Let's make Cashford proud," they'd say and fan out around the theater.

Most of the time, nothing happened. It was just a regular screening of a regular movie. Or at least as regular as anything by Oona Cashford can be.

But every once in a while, in a little theater along a forgotten Main Street or a second-run cineplex tucked back in an otherwise abandoned strip mall, the lights would flicker on after the end of the movie, and there would be one fewer patron than there was at the start. This, it must be emphasized, was much to the delight of fans everywhere.

"You've got to want it bad enough," they'd always say, "or you won't ever be chosen. The movie won't let you in."

And if you're going to disappear into any film, *Sister Skin Savior* is certainly a good one to pick. Oona Cashford's penultimate feature can be summed up with two words: sinisterly sublime. There's been no film quite like it, not before or since.

The story is difficult to describe, most of it communicated wordlessly through long shots of abandoned Rust Belt buildings and billowing fires set for no reason, but the plot—if that's what you could call it—goes something like this: a forlorn woman stalks her philandering husband's new lover and becomes determined not just to outwit her but to *become* her. To climb into her skin and merge with her, flesh and bone and all.

In a way, this reflects Cashford's own obsession with film itself.

"She never stopped fixating on this idea of assimilating into it." Grace pursed her lips, a darkness suddenly clouding her eyes. "Escaping this world was her ultimate dream."

It's worth mentioning that this film was the last collaboration between Oona Cashford and Grace Oliver.

"I couldn't stick around and watch her unravel any longer," Grace told us, and then said no more about it. She didn't say much else at all, eventually excusing herself to the restroom and not returning to answer any more of our questions.

As it turns out, Cashford wasn't the only one unraveling. Her fans were right behind her. They soon began disappearing from screenings across the country. Just here and there, one or two at a time, the kind of lonely people nobody would even notice were missing at first.

When asked where she thought they had gone, Oona would give an odd sort of smile.

"They got there before me," she'd say, a little wistfully.

The Girl with the Gruesome Heart

Oona Cashford's final feature film was released in only six locations nationwide. At the time, there was far more of a demand for it—the arthouse theaters in particular always loved to play her latest movies, even if only in midnight screenings. But Oona was very specific about her choice.

"That's the right number," she said in interviews at the time. "Any more than that, and it just wouldn't be safe."

At that point, of course, nobody knew it was her last feature. Looking back, however, it seems inevitable.

The film itself was a throwback to the kind of goofy, gimmicky productions from her early days. It was set in an ancient estate dressed up like a Hammer production, balsa wood castle and all. Cashford had replaced Grace Oliver with a lookalike actress who irked the director repeatedly throughout production, mostly because she wasn't Grace, and all Oona wanted was Grace. Even so, the new actress did a passable enough job, spending the bulk of the story running away from ghosts and goblins and screaming her pretty little head off.

The audiences in all six locations screamed their heads off too. On opening night—the only night, as it later turned out—they could barely be contained. They tossed popcorn at the screens, and they did callbacks at the characters, and they had such a rollicking good time that the theater owners were pleased as punch that they'd been so lucky to score the film.

That is, until the film was over.

Because when the lights came up, every patron in the theater was gone.

Devourer

After the disappearances of six auditoriums full of fans, nobody would risk financing Oona Cashford's future films. She didn't seem too surprised by this.

"Still, you've got to take risks as an artist," she said, as if her fans' lives were all part of the cost of being a storyteller.

Her next film was a self-financed return to her roots, a short with a running time of only fifteen minutes. It was another ghost story with many of her usual hallmarks: a girl in distress, a world ready to devour her, and absolutely no way out.

It would have been interesting to hear Oona's own commentary on what she intended with the film's dark themes, but by the time of its release, she'd already pulled a vanishing act of her own. So far as anyone can tell, she was in a private screening room, hunkered down alone as she viewed one of her earlier films. (Fans debate whether it was *Sister Skin Savior* or *Menagerie of Death*. Most people go with *Sister Skin Savior* since Grace starred in it, and Oona never stopped talking about her, even after their split.)

What we know for sure: nobody ever saw Oona Cashford come back out of that room.

A perfunctory search was conducted, but at this point, the authorities didn't expect to find anything. After all, when someone disappeared during an Oona Cashford movie, you never found anything again.

A few months after Oona was filed away as a cold case, Grace Oliver did a television interview about her former collaborator. A partial transcript appears below.

> INTERVIEWER: Are you aware of Oona Cashford's current whereabouts?
>
> GRACE: If I knew, don't you think I'd be out there trying to find her? Trying to bring her home?
>
> INTERVIEWER: You two were no longer working together. Why does this case still interest you?
>
> GRACE: We weren't working together, that's true. But that doesn't mean I didn't care about Oona. I wished nothing but the best for her. (*A long, anguished pause.*) I always wanted the best for her.
>
> INTERVIEWER: Do you have any theories about where she went?
>
> GRACE: (*shaking her head, not making eye contact*) She had some wild ideas, I'll tell you that much. And she had places she wanted to go.
>
> INTERVIEWER: Like where?
>
> GRACE: Like the movies. It was the only place she ever wanted to be.

INTERVIEWER: Did she want you to join her?

GRACE: You could say that.

INTERVIEWER: And what did you tell her?

GRACE: I told her that I loved her, but I couldn't follow her.

INTERVIEWER: Now that she's vanished, you must be happy that you didn't stick around.

GRACE: I'm not happy about any of this.

(*Grace abruptly removes her microphone and walks off stage.*)

Untitled #2

Nobody really knows where this film came from. Despite no one having seen Oona in nearly a year, film canisters started appearing at small theaters across the country. At first, they were wholly ignored, with proprietors suspecting the movie was simply the product of hopeful indie filmmakers, desperate to get their latest projects seen any way they could. It wasn't until someone actually watched it that they realized it was Oona's work, another short film, this one focusing for an uncomfortably long time on a shadowy woman's face as it slowly decays into nothing.

What Does It Mean? a few of the headlines at the time asked, but when Oona didn't reappear to answer their question, most critics simply moved on, deeming it another useless stunt in a career chock-full of them. By this time, the vanishing fans were considered nothing but a hoax, despite the hundreds of cases still tucked away in dusty filing cabinets across America. But then again, this shouldn't be so surprising—it's always easier to forget than it is to remember.

But Grace didn't forget, and she didn't see any of this as a stunt. She saw it as a message. And after years of running and years of regret, she finally heeded the call. Shortly after our interview with her, she attended a screening of this particular short film at a rundown movie theater in Manhattan, offering to introduce it and even do a Q&A afterward.

"I'll be glad to help out," she told the theater owner. "Anything to honor Oona."

As promised, she introduced the film, trying her best to explain Oona. As though anyone could really explain Oona. Then she sat in the front row to watch the film. It wasn't a long one, but that didn't matter. She was there when the lights went out, and she was gone when they came back up again.

Nobody saw her vanish, but then they never see them vanish, do they?

The audience filed out solemnly after the film, no Q&A session, no special presentation at all, not without Grace, the only living person who might have been able to understand Oona Cashford. But now they doubted if Grace Oliver was among the living herself.

However, if you asked them, they'd tell you there was one thing they heard as the door to the lobby swung shut behind them. It was a small moment, something a few of them might not have heard at all.

A tiny crystalline laugh that echoed down the aisle and ricocheted off the balcony seats.

A laugh that sounded like freedom.

Untitled #3

It was starting to become a habit. Oona Cashford's short films, the ones that nobody could explain, making their way to tiny movie theaters in every desolate corner of the country.

The same as before, this particular short appeared out of nowhere, although to be fair, it's not much of a film to speak of. It runs a mere five minutes, a paltry production compared to her previous works, as if her instincts were dwindling away. As if Oona herself was dwindling away. Perhaps wherever she went, there isn't much film stock left in the ether.

On a positive note, there were no reports of anybody vanishing during a screening of this film. But that's what's so strange about it; there's no report of anyone who remembers ever seeing the film.

Not even us.

We've tried, of course. We're sure we set up the projector to play it. In fact, we're sure we sat down and watched this film at least four or five times. But when it's over, and the screen goes blank as a fresh paper, we can't remember a single frame of what we saw. We don't even remember where we've been for the past five minutes. It's as if we barely remember ourselves.

Afterwards, though, we can't quite get settled. We wander the halls of our homes like the brooding ghosts in one of Cashford's films. We keep thinking that maybe we don't belong here.

That maybe there's somewhere else that's waiting for us.

Last Dance

Oona Cashford's final film is hardly a film at all. It's no more than static. Thirteen minutes of it, looping over and over again.

Like the previous two shorts, it seemed to be conjured out of thin air, appearing on theater doorsteps when nobody was looking. The only difference is this one came with a title on the side of the film cannisters. *Last Dance*, written in the prettiest cursive letters you've ever seen.

We've watched this film. We've viewed it over and over again, always desperate to decipher its message. If it even has a message. If any of Oona's films have a message. She didn't stick around long enough for us to find out.

But one thing we found, especially late at night, especially when we're alone: if you keep staring into the white noise of this final film, if you keep listening to the purring hiss of that dubious soundtrack, then maybe you'll finally see something. It's faint and it's distant, but if you're persistent, it's there. The shape of her, the shape of everything. Then maybe you'll finally understand. Maybe we can all understand what she's been trying to tell us since the beginning.

Thank you for attending this retrospective of filmmaker Oona Cashford. If you're still with us, please don't be too disappointed. We promise it's not too late.

Because Oona's films are still here, still patient in their metal canisters, ready to be unspooled, ready for you to try again, eager for you to become part of them.

After all, films like hers will always be waiting.

AUTHOR NOTES

Just a few notes directly from the authors about their stories, plus short bios and where to follow each for more of their work.

Andrew Cull

"Carly's Wish"

I've always loved two-hander thrillers. I love the intricate interplay between the two protagonists. How characters are drawn, and then redrawn over the course of a short scene. How two-handers play with form, with your expectations, and will often hold a sting in the tail.

I'd had the rough idea for "Carly's Wish" rattling around in the haunted corridors of my brain for a while. I knew that I wanted to write something that explored the secondary victims of an unsolved crime: a family or family member grieving the loss of a loved one while trying to find answers and closure, but I wanted to do it in a way I hadn't read before.

The story is in part inspired by the Dutch thriller *The Vanishing*, *Hitchcock's Rope*, and by the short stories of Robert Bloch and Richard Matheson. Thank you to John and Shane for inviting me to be a part of this fantastic anthology, and thank you for giving my story a read. I hope you dig, "Carly's Wish."

Andrew Cull is an award-winning writer and horror director. He's the author of *Bones*, *Remains,* and, most recently, *The Cockroach King*. His story collection *Bones* has been described as "a masterclass in emotional cinematic horror fiction." Andrew lives in Melbourne, Australia. He loves horror and Hitchcock, and, like you, he's not easily scared. Follow Andy on Twitter: @andrewcull.

Shane Hawk

"Skin Maps"

So many of us teachers operate underneath the umbrella of what are called "essential questions" during our lessons. These are big-picture questions we want the students to be able to answer once we finish. This story started out as the essential question: As a Native, how important is it to know where you belong?

When I began my first draft, I had just finished reading Marcie R. Rendon's *Murder on the Red River*. The protagonist, Cash Blackbear, was an adopted Ojibwe woman torn from her kin at an early age. In her author's note, Rendon makes her readers reflect on Indian boarding schools and how, before the Indian Child Welfare Act of 1978 (ICWA) was put into place, Native children were stripped away from their families and tribes, placed into adoption agencies, and from there non-Natives adopted them. Many Native children were exploited as unpaid farm hands, essentially slave laborers, by their new adoptive families, too.

At the same time, political discussions regarding the ICWA were heating up, and the Supreme Court reviewed a lawsuit (*Brackeen v. Haaland*) in November 2022 that could overturn the ICWA. [SCOTUS makes their final decision in June 2023.] This scary thought influenced me to write this near-future dystopian story as speculation as to what could happen with its overturn and how far someone would go—through sheer desperation—to discover their tribe, the land to which they belong.

Editor's Note: The Supreme Court on June 15, 2023 declined to disturb a federal law governing the process for placing Native American children in foster or adoptive homes with Native American families, rejecting constitutional challenges to the law.

Shane Hawk, a member of the Cheyenne and Arapaho Tribes of Oklahoma, is a history teacher by day and a horror writer by night. He entered the horror scene with his first publication, *Anoka: A Collection of Indigenous Horror*, in October 2020. Hawk is also the co-editor of *Never Whistle at Night*, an anthology of Indigenous dark fiction that Penguin Random House will publish in September 2023. He lives in San Diego with his beautiful wife, Tori. Learn more by visiting shanehawk.com.

Jonathan Janz

"The Third Shannon"

"The Third Shannon" probably came about because when I was a little kid I was a bit ornery. Between the ages of five and eleven I'd stay up late to watch scrambled versions of pay-TV channels like Showtime and Cinemax. I'd strain my eyes to see all the adult stuff that was happening in those movies, and on the rare occasions we got free trials of the channels…well, the elementary-school version of me was very happy. "The Third Shannon" is about a guy who never grew out of that fixation, who instead took his eagerness to an unhealthy level and let it consume his adult life. Incidentally, I knew a guy with this obsession in college (and no, it wasn't me). He wasn't quite as extreme as the protagonist of my story, and I haven't seen him in years. But I wouldn't be at all surprised if I found out the guy has a room dedicated to the actresses mentioned in this tale. Especially Shannon Tweed.

Jonathan Janz is a novelist, screenwriter, and film teacher. He's represented for film and television by Ryan Lewis (executive producer of *Bird Box*). His work has been championed by authors like Josh Malerman, Caroline Kepnes, Stephen Graham Jones, Joe R. Lansdale, and Brian Keene. His ghost story *The Siren and the Specter* was selected as a Goodreads Choice nominee for Best Horror. Additionally, his novels *Children of the Dark* and *The Dark Game* were chosen by Booklist and Library Journal as Top Ten Horror Books of the Year. Jonathan's main interests are his wonderful wife and his three amazing children.

Shane D. Keene

"Morbidologies"

The number 13. The whole reason this poem came into being is because I insisted—morbidly, one could say—on having thirteen pieces in it. We came up one short, and John said, "There you go, you want thirteen, it's on you now."

At first I made a false start, penning a piece about a scent so fresh in my olfactory memory I couldn't stomach finishing it. Someday you will experience my version of rat salad, but it needs to stew for a while yet. So I made this little feel-good verse about a curious individual, obsessed with murder and the myriad ways to commit it. It's one of those poems that make people look at me and go, "What the fuck is wrong with you?"

Those are my favorite ones to write.

Shane D. Keene is a poet, author, and musician. His poems and stories have appeared in several publications including *Chiral Mad 5* from Written Backwards and *Picnic in the Graveyard* and *Paranormal Contact*, both from Cemetery Gates. His poetry collection *Moth Frenzy* will release sometime in 2023. He lives in Springfield, Oregon, with his wife Rebecca, an Australian Koolie, and a tiny black skeleton named Shadow. that once looked like a Pomeranian.

Gwendolyn Kiste

"The Eleven Films of Oona Cashford"

The films of William Castle have always fascinated me, ever since I was a very young horror fan. The over-the-top theatrics and the wonderfully weird gimmicks, including his electrical buzzers on theater seats for *The Tingler* and his Illusion-O special glasses for seeing spirits during *13 Ghosts*, encapsulate everything I love about the genre. Horror has such a reputation for being dark and dour, but it can also be unbelievably lively and fun, and Castle's films really captured that unique kind of macabre magic.

I wish very much that we had a real-life Oona Cashford, a female filmmaker who incorporated gimmicks into her work during the 1960s and 1970s and garnered a huge following in the process. Unfortunately, women have too often been cut out of the arts, so historically, there haven't been nearly enough female directors. On a positive note, things are shifting for the better, albeit slowly, so maybe that auteur is still out there, and we'll all get to enjoy her monster movies one day. For now, the best I can do is to create such characters in my own strange little fictional worlds. Perhaps, if we're lucky, we can conjure our own Oona into existence.

Gwendolyn Kiste is the three-time Bram Stoker Award-winning author of *The Rust Maidens*, *Reluctant Immortals, Boneset & Feathers*, *And Her Smile Will Untether the Universe*, *Pretty Marys All in a Row*, and *The Invention of Ghosts*. Her short fiction and nonfiction have appeared in *Nightmare Magazine*, *Best American Science Fiction and Fantasy*, *Lit Hub*, *Vastarien*, Tor Nightfire, Titan Books, *Black Static*, *The Dark*, and *LampLight*, among others. Originally from Ohio, she now resides on an abandoned horse farm outside of Pittsburgh with her husband, their excitable calico cat, and not nearly enough ghosts. Find her online at gwendolynkiste.com.

Eric LaRocca

"In Mourning, She Wakes Again"

It's no secret that I'm very vocal on social media about how close I am with my mother. A dedicated admirer of horror cinema and fiction, my mother was the one who first introduced me to the genre at a young age. I'll never forget the terror I felt while first watching *Creature from the Black Lagoon* at the age of nine years old, imagining webbed feet creeping down the corridor outside my bedroom late at night. Although I've yet to forgive her for the nightmares, my mother has always remained my strongest supporter and my most dedicated fan.

When I was first approached to write a piece for *Morbidologies*, I desperately wanted to write a story that explored the relationship between a devoted mother and her deceased son. Given the theme of the anthology, I wanted this story to explore the darkest parts of human obsession and our social concepts surrounding death. Moreover, I wanted this story to be elegant and I wanted it to appear to readers as if it takes place in a time that's not outright recognizable as the present. I wanted this piece to take place in a vague time period in order to really unsettle readers and make them more uncomfortable with the subject matter at play.

Fiction that makes us uncomfortable is usually the kind of fiction we remember. I hope I've offered you something unique and truly memorable today.

Eric LaRocca (he/they) is the Bram Stoker Award®-nominated and Splatterpunk Award-winning author of several works of horror and dark fiction, including the viral sensation, *Things Have Gotten*

Worse Since We Last Spoke. A lover of luxury fashion and an admirer of European musical theatre, Eric can often be found roaming the streets of his home city, Boston, MA, for inspiration. For more information, please follow @hystericteeth on Twitter/Instagram or visit ericlarocca.com.

Beverley Lee

"The Fall of Felix Ellerby"

I've always been in love with the Gothic, so a chance to set this one in the Victorian era was too tempting to resist. Give me a gloom-drenched manor house and a family, add in a pivotal turning point and sit back and watch it all burn (figuratively). I never plot, I just run with a story idea and see where it takes me. Felix came to me with a past, but at the point of starting I didn't know what that past was, or what he had done. Or what he still does. It was a journey of discovery as I unpeeled his layers and uncovered what he was capable of. The echoes of childhood events/traumas follow us all the days of our lives, and Felix is no exception. But what he did, he did for love, so don't judge him too fiercely by the time you turn the final page.

Apart from the obvious Gothic attraction, this story was a chance for me to flex my writer's wings in a slightly different way. It pays homage to Edgar Allen Poe, the foundational guiding light (or should that be darkness?) of the mysterious and the macabre. Playing in such an inspirational sandbox was indeed an honor.

Beverley Lee is the bestselling author of the Gabriel Davenport series (*The Making of Gabriel Davenport, A Shining in the Shadows* and *The Purity of Crimson*), *The Ruin of Delicate Things, The House of Little Bones*, and *The Sum of Your Flesh*. She is also co-author of *Crimson is the Night*, a vampire novelette, with Nicole Eigener. Her shorter fiction has been included in works from Cemetery Gates Media, Kandisha Press, Brigids Gate Press and Off Limits Press. In thrall to the written word from an early age, especially the darker side of fiction, she believes that the very best story is the one you have to tell. Supporting fellow authors is also her passion and she is actively involved in social media and writers' groups. You can visit her online at beverleylee.com (where you'll find a free dark and twisted short story download) or on Instagram (@theconstantvoice) and Twitter (@constantvoice).

Chad Lutzke

"3:00 Meating"

Like most writers, I have a file filled with years of story ideas. Everything from dreams to photos, random thoughts, and bizarre news articles. One such article piqued my interest about three or four years ago, when I read about some people reporting they'd seen a cloaked and hooded figure emerge from some nearby woods that sat on the edge of an elementary school playground. The figure crept from the woods, then set a large piece of raw meat on the playground. As a bonus, there was an accompanying picture of the figure—in all its grainy and blurred glory—setting the meat down.

The article was the prompts of all prompts. The king prompt! I knew one day I'd use that in a story.

Unfortunately, about a year later, I saw another article stating they believed some local kids were merely recording a short film and the cloaked figure with the meat was part of it. I try to forget I read that second article, that the incident still remains a mystery, and we'll never know why a cloaked figure fed raw meat to a children's playground.

Chad Lutzke lives in Battle Creek, Michigan, with his wife and children. For over two decades, he has been a contributor to several different outlets in the independent music and film scene, offering articles, reviews, and artwork. He's had several dozen short stories published, and is known for his heartfelt approach to the dark side of humanity with books such as *Of Foster Homes & Flies, Wallflower, Stirring the Sheets, Skullface Boy, The Pale White, Three-Smile Mile,* and *The Neon Owl*. Lutzke's work has been praised by Jack Ketchum, Richard Chizmar, Joe R. Lansdale, Stephen Graham Jones, and his own mother.

J. Daniel Stone

"Raging in the Dark"

This my return to fiction writing. After losing more than two years of my life due to divorce, the pandemic and starting over, I really thought I'd never write again, because once you get into a pattern of not being creative, you can easily remain that way. Spiraling downward is far easier than finding the strength to climb out of that said spiral. But when Taff asked me to write a new story for him…that was the kick in the ass that I needed to be creative again.

"Raging in the Dark" is set around characters that are all in my fourth novel, *Daubed in Darkness*, but I really don't know the timeline of when this would have taken place *within* the novel. Probably somewhere between the second half and the end of the book. "Raging in the Dark" is my love letter to artists and the extremes that they go to in order to create. Art is not limited to painting and sketching, it can be anything, if you›re the one creating it.

What I loved about this story most was bringing in a brand-new character (not in the novel) and introducing her to three main characters from the novel. What happens when you put too many pious creators in a room together? Do their egos get in the way? Or do they take each other to new and exciting heights? Raging in the Dark may or may not answer those questions. Also, for some background, the story is set *during the pandemic* (and its ubiquitous shutdowns).

NYC born and raised **J. Daniel Stone** writes urban horror with a queer focus. He sold his first story when he was 22-years-old and has since written three novels (*The Absence of Light, Blood Kiss* and *Stations of Shadow*), and the forthcoming *Daubed in Darkness*, as well as a short story collection (*Lovebites & Razorlines*) and a novella (*I Can Taste The Blood*). He writes under a pseudonym to keep the wolves at bay. Visit him at www.SolitarySpiral.com and all socials @SolitarySpiral.

John F.D. Taff

"The Great Momentum of Doubt"

Anthologies often do not work out the way you think they will when you first set off to create one with a smile on your face and a song in your heart. Among the many things that can and do go wrong, sometimes the authors you want to work with, the authors you invite, all don't make it to the finish line with you. It happens. Life intervenes, and there's no time. Creative differences, all that stuff. So, when Shane and I found ourselves two stories down from the number we'd planned for, Shane suggested a story from me. Contrary to how it may seem, I don't think of these projects as vehicles for my own work. But I had one that fit, and here we are.

"The Great Momentum of Doubt" grew from thinking about how great tragedies sometimes make it hard to move on, to move away from them. Often, though, it's not the entire tragedy that occupies people's thoughts—that's just too big to process—but small, nagging details. People can obsess over certain details about horrible things that don't seem to add up or even matter.

But sometimes they do.

John F.D. Taff is the multiple Bram Stoker Award-nominated author of *The End in All Beginnings* and *The Fearing*. His short stories and novellas have appeared in innumerable magazines and anthologies over the last thirty years. Peter Straub once tweeted that he was "mighty cool," which Taff will undoubtedly have engraved on his tombstone. Taff's recent work can be seen in *The Bad Book*, the anthology he edited for Bleeding Edge Books, and *Dark Stars* from Tor/Nightfire, the anthology he edited and contributed to. His work has also appeared in anthologies such as *Gutted, Behold, Shadows Over Main Street 2, Orphans of Bliss, Lullabies for Suffering* and *Human Monsters*. New work will appear soon in projects that haven't been announced yet. You can follow Taff on Twitter @johnfdtaff.

AUTHOR NOTES

Sonora Taylor

"Pluck"

"Pluck" is a story that comes from a lifetime of being a little swarthy. From a young age I was blessed with thick eyebrows, sideburns, and then in adulthood, a light mustache and short spiky chin hairs that seem to multiply when I pluck them out, like the heads of a hydra.

While Marleigh's story is much more horrific than mine, I was inspired by my overall relationship with facial and eyebrow hair. My tweezers and I have a date almost every day when it comes to stubborn chin hairs. One of my anxiety tics is constantly pulling at hairs I feel under my chin with my fingers. I also had a brief hair-pulling habit in middle school, to the point where I once horrified my friend in home room as I pulled out a good-sized chunk of hair while we listened to announcements. Unlike Marleigh though, I'm doing okay with my eyebrows—probably because they're at the point where they're barely growing back since I've waxed and plucked them for going on twenty years.

One small horror story does involve my eyebrows, though; and it was also a source of inspiration for "Pluck." My mother often tweezed my eyebrows for me when I was in high school, since she had more practice than I did. One evening, she was plucking away like normal, when I suddenly felt a sensation as if a rip cord were being pulled from my eyebrow. Her eyes widened and her mouth dropped as the hair revealed itself to be at least half an inch long once plucked. We both had a good laugh about it, so naturally, years later I needed to turn it into something horrifying.

Thanks so much for reading "Pluck." I hope it made your skin crawl in all the right ways.

Sonora Taylor is the award-winning author of several short stories and books, including *Little Paranoias: Stories, Seeing Things, and Without Condition.* She also co-edited *Diet Riot: A Fatterpunk Anthology* with Nico Bell. Her stories have been published by Rooster Republic Press, Tenebrous Press, Cemetery Gates Media, Ghost Orchid Press, and others. She is an active member of the Horror Writers Association and serves on the board of directors of Scares That Care. She lives in Arlington, Virginia, with her husband and a rescue dog. You can find her online at sonorawrites.com, on Twitter at @sonorawrites, and on Instagram (where she mostly posts food pictures) at @sonorataylor.

Wendy N. Wagner

"No God of Bread or Debts"

When I was eight, my dad bought a fish tank and stocked it with all the classic aquarium fish: fancy-tailed guppies, neon zetas, and of course, an algae eater to help keep everything clean. Of all the fish, the algae eater did the best. It grew slowly but steadily, and once it hit four inches long, other fish began disappearing from the tank. An anxious creature, it hid in the corners of the tank, mostly lurking behind the air filter, and it would race away if it caught a glimpse of any humans. At one point, one of my friends became convinced that the algae eater was possessed by a demon. She would pray over the tank and tape up pictures of crosses around its sides. The algae eater did not appreciate this treatment, but continued its quiet, nervous life for several more years. The last six months or so of its existence, it had the tank to itself, which it seemed to appreciate. It spent more time hanging out in the center of the tank, rubbing its belly across the larger rocks and fluttering its fins through the plants.

After the algae eater's death, my family stopped keeping fish. My father lost his interest in fish entirely, and even stopped taking me fishing. My world moved out of the orbit of aquatic creatures, and they mostly faded from my mind until about a year ago, when I happened to pick up the book Stronghold, a biography about Guido Rahr, one of the world's foremost fly fishermen and salmon conservationists. His stories about duck-eating taimen, scheming sturgeon, and the ancient beauty of migratory fishes made me remember the hours I spent watching the fish in our aquarium. I started reading more about fish and wondering about their amazing adaptations to our world.

When I was invited to submit to *Morbidologies*, I immediately thought of Rahr. Here was a man who at times had cut himself off from his family, who had risked his life at the hands of Russian mobsters, who had journeyed to some of the most remote and dangerous rivers on the planet because of an obsession with fish. What would his evil mirror-image be like? What would they be driven to do? As soon as I thought it, I knew I had to write that story.

Wendy N. Wagner is a writer and Hugo award-winning editor. Her novels include the forthcoming cosmic horror novel *The Creek Girl* (Tor Nightfire, 2025), *The Deer Kings*, and the Locus best-selling *An Oath of Dogs*. Her short stories, essays, and poems have appeared in seventy-some publications, running the gamut from horror to environmental literature. She is also the editor-in-chief of *Nightmare Magazine* and the managing/senior editor of *Lightspeed*. She lives in Oregon with her very understanding family, two large cats, and a Muppet disguised as a dog. You can find her at winniewoohoo.com.

Craig Wallwork

"Beyond the Red Door"

There was a point sometime last year where I developed toothache caused by bruxism. The pain was tantamount to injecting my gums with Sriracha and did a great job at slowly killing the tooth from the root up. Around this same time, I fell out of love with contemporary literature. The two are not related. The thing is, all my literary heroes are dead. Or if not dead, the writers I admire and gravitate to were sinking under the weight of airport fiction. But that hunger to be inspired remained in me during those long nights in agony. Without books to distract me, I leant on movies, getting my fix from Giallo giants like Argento and Bava, as well as horror auteurs like Julia Ducournau, Joko Anwar, Travis Stevens, and Vincent Grimshaw. But two movies that ignited the powder trail to my darkened heart during this period were Adrian Lyme's 1990 psychological horror *Jacob's Ladder* and Carpenter's Lovecraftian inspired *In the Mouth of Madness*.

That fascination where creatures and the walking dead appear in reality and push the protags into morbid territory was something I wanted to explore. So, with a rhythm set by Nick Cave, and a persistent throbbing in my jaw, I turned the handle and crossed the threshold into "Beyond the Red Door," a story that blurs the line between reality and otherworldliness and tells of a man obsessed with antique surgical equipment. That this story is now in your hands is a pleasant consequence to a horrible time. The tooth that kept me up at night is still in my head, awaiting the dentist's pliers as and when I conjure up the courage to make that appointment. It's my hope that this story remains with you, too, and like that tooth, keeps you awake in the night and haunts you long into the morning.

Craig Wallwork is the author of the horror thriller series, *Bad People, Labyrinth of the Dolls*, and *The Ghost of Stormer Hill*. He's written two other novels, *Heart of Glass*, and *The Sound of Loneliness*, as well as the short story collections *Human Tenderloin, Quintessence of Dust*, and *Gory Hole*. His stories—many of which feature in various anthologies and magazines both in the U.K. and U.S.—have been nominated three times for the Pushcart Prize. He is also the co-host of the horror podcast, *Session 10*. You can find out more about him at www.craigwallwork.com.

ACKNOWLEDGMENTS

John

I'd like to thank first and foremost Shane D. Keene, my co-editor. Shane has been a huge supporter of mine since the early days. He's grown into quite the poet, and his exposure to wide swathes of horror through his literary reviews and podcasts made him a natural for me to co-edit an anthology for the first time. I particularly want to thank him for being keen (hah), inquisitive, and easy to work with.

Thanks again to another great friend, D. Alexander Ward, the publisher at Bleeding Edge Books. I worked with him on *The Bad Book*, so this time around just seemed natural. Thanks to Todd Keisling for designing the book and to Christine M. Scott for the cover art. It all came together in a spectacular package.

Thanks to the great authors who took the ride

with us this time. We appreciate the hard work. Can't wait to hear back from readers!

Finally, thanks to my wonderful wife, Deborah, who allows me to do this stuff. And as always to my kids, Harry, Sam, and Molly.

Shane

I have to follow suit here and thank John F.D. Taff, my friend and co-editor. Once upon a time I said, I have a crazy idea, and he said, that *is* crazy. Let's talk. His trust and mentorship are what's really crazy and most important to me. This is a great book because we made it together with all these wonderful authors. It's an amazing one because John knows how to make those happen and he shared some of his experience with me.

Thanks to our publisher, D. Alexander Ward, and his belief in the idea. And for his dedication to pure fucking awesome production. I knew when John said he was our guy, we were in the best of hands.

Mostly, thanks to Rebecca, who saved me and gave me reasons to keep going even when I kept trying to throw them all away.

www.ingramcontent.com/pod-product-compliance
Ingram Content Group UK Ltd.
Pitfield, Milton Keynes, MK11 3LW, UK
UKHW041636190726
13854UKWH00006B/2528